PRESS

By
Betsy Reavley

Print ISBN : 978-1-912604-25-8

Also by Betsy Reavley
Beneath The Watery Moon
Carrion
The Quiet Ones
The Optician's Wife
Frailty

Praise For Betsy Reavely

"An addictive, compelling read that pushed me well out of my comfort zone - if you like disturbingly twisty plot lines and dark characters then this is definitely the read for you." *Lisa Hall, Author of the best selling psychological thriller Between You and Me*

"The Optician's Wife is a stylish, brilliantly crafted thriller which really delivers. A very real sense of creeping dread, combined with intelligent, finely drawn characters, had me turning the pages late into the night. This one will linger with you, long after the book is finished. Reavley has delivered a masterclass and deserves to be up there with the best in the business." *L J Ross - Bestselling author of The DCI Ryan books.*

"I love discovering new authors especially one who can shock and surprise me like this as it doesn't happen very often!" *Joanne Robertson - My Chestnut Reading Tree*

"Don't you just love it when you pick up a book and it blows you away, well Betsy Reavley has managed to do just that with a book that's absolutely filled with suspense and intrigue." *Lorraine Rugman - The Book Review Cafe*

"This was a fantastic book and one I knew from the first chapter it was going to keep me enthralled reading it." *Leona - Goodreads Reviewer*

"Wow! What a stunning book. Draws you in, spins you a line and boom! you've got it completely wrong. Loved it. So clever." *MetLineReader - Goodreads Reviewer*

"This is a book that once you start reading it you won't be able to stop. It is a story that grabs you right from the very beginning." *Joseph Calleja, Relax and Read book Reviews*

"This is true stand-out in the domestic noir genre." *Caroline Matson, Confessions of a Reading Addict*

"Betsy Reavley has reached new heights with this breathtaking book. Child abduction is always a difficult subject and she has totally embraced it in this outstanding book. It will leave you feeling emotionally drained and in awe of this author. Her best book yet, a literary masterpiece" *Anita Waller, best-selling author of 34 Days, Angel and Beautiful*

"Absolutely incredible book, cannot praise it enough. I think it's my best read of 2016." *Emma De Oliveira, an ARC reviewer*

"It went from heart pounding moments to adrenaline rushes where I simply couldn't speak. This is one of my top three books of the year, awesome!" *Susan Hampson - Books From Dusk Till Dawn*

"Reavley has written a stunning thriller which is fast-paced and full of twists and turns. I was completely invested in this narrative, submerged by the tension and gravity of the situation." *Clair Boor - Have Books Will Read*

This book is dedicated to all lost souls

All Day I Hear the Noise of Waters

by James Joyce
All day I hear the noise of waters
Making moan,
Sad as the sea-bird is when, going
Forth alone,
He hears the winds cry to the water's
Monotone.

The grey winds, the cold winds are blowing
Where I go.
I hear the noise of many waters
Far below.
All day, all night, I hear them flowing
To and fro.

* * *

pressure noun

- the force that a liquid or gas produces when it presses against an area
- the act of trying to make someone else do something
- a difficult situation that makes you feel worried or unhappy

The Pica Explorer floor plan

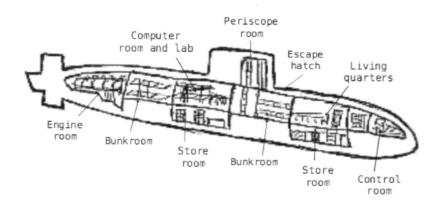

Engine room

Computer room and lab

Periscope room

Escape hatch

Living quarters

Bunk room

Store room

Bunk room

Store room

Control room

Prologue

Day one. Hour 00:00.

'What do you mean, it isn't responding?' I watch the colour drain from his face as the dials on the control panel all began to drop.

'I don't know.' The sweat appears on his brow, reflecting the lights from the dashboard, putting a sheen on his face that makes him appear ghostlike.

'This has never happened before. We are losing power. This isn't meant to be happening.' Swinging around in the chair, he catapults himself towards the radio system and begins the Mayday process.

'This is the captain of The Pica Explorer. We are losing power. Repeat, we are losing power. The vessel is descending. Our position is—'

And just then all the lights go out.

Child

'*You always were a little shit.*' *Her hot breath, which reeked of coffee, was too close to my face for comfort. 'You're an embarrassment.'*

I think I winced before her balled up fist made contact with the side of my head. I knew it was coming even before she had made the decision. That look in her eyes warned me. It was the same look every single time.

'I'm sorry,' I whimpered, my ears ringing from the impact of her thump.

'You are disgusting.' A flicker of spittle left her mouth and landed on my face in a fine spray.

As I remained cowering on the ground, she proceeded to tear the urine-stained sheets off of my bed like a wild animal attacking its prey. The side of my head felt swollen and I was finding it difficult to hear out of the ear she had walloped.

Seconds later she'd wrapped the wet sheets around me and proceeded to drag me down the stairs, the smell of my own urine clogging my nostrils, making it difficult to breathe.

'Get in there!' she screamed as I heard the cellar door open with a creak. Moments later I felt her foot connect with my back and I was tumbling down more stairs, still wrapped in the damp, foul-smelling sheet.

'Now, you can think about what you've done,' she panted from somewhere above before slamming the door closed.

I listened as the key was turned, knowing I was locked in the darkness, alone, until she decided otherwise.

1

At nine years old I knew I shouldn't be wetting the bed. I knew it was disgusting and abnormal but I couldn't help it. My dreams were so terrifying I couldn't stop it happening.

Once in a while I would wake in the night, dripping with sweat and lying in my own wee. On those occasions I'd remove the sheets, put them in the bottom of my laundry basket and sneak onto the landing to fetch some fresh ones so she would never know.

But unfortunately I didn't always wake. Sometimes I would sleep right through, tossing and turning, a prisoner to my own imagination. And then the birds would start to sing and the sunshine would creep through the curtains. On mornings like that I wished I wasn't alive. I knew Mummy would soon appear and discover my dirty accident and there was nothing I could do about it.

The Pica Explorer

Day one. Hour 00:05.

You have never known real darkness until you have been deep underwater. It is not like the blackness you experience when you stand in a field in the dark. It is much more alive than that. The darkness behaves like a cloak that wraps itself around everything and you can almost feel it crawling on your skin.

There is a strange silence from those of us in the control room. Nobody screams. We remain in the brooding darkness with only the sound of our breathing reminding us that we are still alive.

'The backup power will kick in.' Patrick, the captain, speaks with faux confidence. 'This machine is built to withstand the depths.'

No one responds. We just stay still knowing that we are sinking further and further below the surface and into the dark water.

I can feel the pressure building all around us and my heart, which thumps violently in my chest, threatens to explode at any moment.

I hear the squeak from the castors on Patrick's chair but can still see nothing.

'When will the lights come back on?' Susie's quiet, almost childlike, voice cuts through the blackness.

'Any moment.' Patrick clears his throat just as blue light fills the space.

'Frank!' I rush to the door and call for him. 'How far down can we go?' I turn and ask a moment before Frank appears.

'What the fuck is going on?' Frank stands tall looking down on us.

'We will land on the ocean floor soon enough.' Patrick speaks with authority.

'How soon?' Susie's voice has risen an octave higher.

'We won't sink deeper than a couple of hundred metres,' Fiona says and then clears her throat.

'What about the pressure?' Susie squeaks again.

'Stop whining, Susie,' Frank barks. 'I demand someone tells me what is going on?'

'The sub has lost power and we are descending.' Patrick still fiddles with the dials on the panel hoping to fix the problem.

'But we will all be crushed.' We all hear the tears in Susie's voice.

'No, we won't,' Fiona says calmly. 'The ocean floor is not that deep here. There is no danger of us sinking to the crush depth.'

'The backup power has kicked in.' Patrick turns to Frank gesturing to the blue light.

'Then we can start climbing back up to the surface?' Susie's wide eyes look hopefully at Fiona.

'I'm afraid not. The backup power only feeds the air and lighting.' Fiona throws a look at Patrick.

'How long will it last?' Frank suddenly doesn't seem so sure of himself.

'Well, we've never had to rely on it before...' Patrick returns to the control panel and begins flicking switches and dials again.

'But they heard our call, didn't they?' My throat feels dry as the words force themselves out.

No one responds, instead we all find ourselves gazing out of the front window at the wondrous underwater world we are now a part of. Still the submarine is drifting downwards, and above us the light from the sky is fading further and further away.

'I'm going for a piss.' Frank pushes his way past Susie and through the narrow doorway that leads to the living quarters in the sub, looking for any excuse to leave the room.

I mouth the word 'arsehole' to Susie and wink, getting her to smile if only temporarily.

'So what do we do?' Fiona turns to Patrick hoping for a simple explanation. But underneath she knows that the captain is as lost as the rest of us.

'Well, we need to go into the engine room.' Patrick is stoic as he stands up in the confined space, careful not to bang his head on the low ceiling.

He is a tall gangly man and every bit the quintessential scientist. His mousey brown hair is too long and always scruffy, as is his beard that has many grey hairs interspersed with the ginger ones.

'I'll come with you.' Fiona follows him out, leaving just Susie and me alone.

'This is serious, isn't it.' She looks out into the vast expanse of ocean, which consumes us.

'Yes. Yes, it is.' I put my hand on her shoulder and try to ignore the repetitive thump in my chest that is making it difficult to breathe.

Zara

When I got the call I nearly fell off my seat. I'd been dreaming an opportunity like this would come along at some point in my career.

'Yes, yes, absolutely. I'd be honoured.' I had to put my hand over my mouth to stop an excited squeal from escaping down the phone. 'I will be there. Thank you so much for this chance. You won't regret it.'

Putting the phone down, I then proceeded to do a happy dance around my small London apartment.

I'd been living in Dalston for four years, scraping a living as an assistant director on a very low budget television show, which was only shown late at night on a poxy satellite channel that no one had ever heard of.

Cops and Robbers was a programme that followed police officers around the dingy parts of London, as they arrested youths and petty criminals. It was aimed at the lowest common denominator but it paid the bills and had been my first break into television. Beggars couldn't be choosers and although I had graduated from The London Film School with a master's in film-making, I had to take work where I could get it.

The course had cost a small fortune and meant I had to work my fingers to the bone, living in a cheap shitty flat in Walthamstow and travelling into the city centre to complete my education.

With famous directors such as Michael Mann and Mike Leigh graduating from LFS, I had dreams of becoming an industry hotshot. But real life doesn't always work out the way you hope it will, and soon after I had completed my course, it became quickly apparent to me that there was no easy path to the big league. So when the chance to work on *Cops and Robbers* presented itself, I had no choice but to accept the gig. It was a start, I told myself.

I'd known since I was a teenager that I wanted to get into film. Seeing life through a lens fascinated me and there was something especially alluring about moving picture.

When I'd spotted the chance to work with one of the UK's biggest directors on a feature, I'd put myself forward for the role. Knowing my experience was limited, I didn't fancy my chances very highly, but as my boyfriend always said: if you throw enough shit at the wall eventually some of it will stick. So that's what I did. I went for every single job I could and started to get used to the string of rejections that I received.

Frank Holden, of FH House Films, was an industry giant. He was a producer and a director all rolled into one. His production company was responsible for some of the biggest hits to come out of the UK and he had spent much of his career in LA working with Hollywood megastars.

After applying for the job I didn't expect to get a response but when I was called in for a meeting I nearly fainted. It was unheard of for someone of his stature to consider working with a rookie like me.

All became clear when I showed up at his swanky London offices for the meeting.

The film that he had optioned was unlike any film that had ever been made. It was set in an underwater world and was about a crew of scientists who discovered an alien race living in the ocean, unbeknown to the rest of humanity. The film had started life as a graphic novel, which I'd heard Frank had come across. He'd instantly fallen in love with the concept and decided he wanted to turn the comic into a film.

But, at the time, I didn't know that there was a storm brewing in the industry and Frank Holden was on the brink of losing everything. It seems that a number of young actresses had complained about unwarranted attention and advances from Frank, in return for leading roles in his films as well as their silence.

FH House Films was doing its very best to bury the story, but I soon discovered, from an employee of the firm who was very happy to gossip, that a reporter had gotten hold of the story and was threatening to blow the whole thing open. As a result, the company he had built was holding back from allowing Frank his usual large budget on the feature.

So Frank, who was renowned for being stubborn, decided he would go ahead and produce the film with a much lower budget, which meant nobodies like me were invited to meetings. He was a man who answered to no one.

I didn't care about Frank's wandering hands or his reputation for luring young women into bed. All I cared about was the opportunity to work with a genius in the field. My desire to succeed was second to none.

I can now admit that when I walked into the studio for my first meeting, with his personal assistant, I was shaking like a leaf. I wasn't used to the ultra-modern leather sofas, industrial lighting and the luxury of the building. It was so far removed from the flea-infested bedsit that I called home.

While I sat awkwardly perched on the edge of the sofa waiting to be called in, I grew increasingly aware of the sound my trousers made against the leather. In a corner, behind a large glass desk, sat a secretary with super stylish clothing and her dark hair piled high on her head. She wore brown lipstick that made her pale skin look like that of a china doll. I felt ugly and out of place in her world.

'Zara Golding.' The receptionist fixed me with her cold eyes. 'They will see you now.' And she pointed towards a door on the far side of the room.

Getting up from the sofa and wincing, as my trousers again made a farting noise against the leather material, I straightened my navy jacket and made my way towards the door, which swung open just before I reached it.

'Zara, I'm guessing?' A flamboyant American woman dressed head-to-toe in black put her hand out and shook mine. 'Won't you come in?'

I followed the unknown woman through a brightly lit corridor; her kitten heels clattering on the hardwood floor.

'Frank's just through here. He is super excited to meet you.' I nodded and smiled although I found her statement hard to believe. 'I'm Monica Cherry, Frank's PA,' she explained while leading me into a room with a frosted glass door.

Sitting behind a large desk was Frank. I recognised him instantly. His large frame, small brown eyes and balding head were unmistakable. He didn't smile or say a word. He simply sat looking at me. I didn't know if I should take a seat or speak, or what it was he expected of me.

'Geez, hon, take a seat won't you.' Monica's American drawl echoed around the stark office as she went around the desk and took her seat next to Frank.

I pulled the black leather and steel chair back and sat myself down, being sure to keep my back very straight. *You mustn't slouch* – the words my mother used to say rang in my ears.

'So.' Monica picked up a shiny tablet that was on the desk in front of her and scanned the page.

'You don't have much experience.' Frank spoke suddenly.

'Erm, no.' I shifted in my chair.

'So what are you doing here?' he asked, still staring without blinking.

Unsure how to answer, I looked to Monica for guidance but her eyes remained focused on the tablet. She was not going to help me.

'Well, I… I came because I got a call.' I realised too late how lame I sounded.

'Wrong.' Frank leant forward, knitting his chubby fingers together on the desk in front of him. On his right hand little finger he wore a large gold signet ring. 'You came because you want to work in film.'

'Yes, that's right.'

'But you have no experience.'

'I have a little.'

'*Cops and Robbers?*' he sneered.

I took an instant dislike to the man.

'Yes.'

'You graduated from LFS with distinction,' Monica chipped in, still studying her notes.

'That's right.'

'So you're smart enough. You have a bit of talent.' Frank sat back in his chair and rubbed his stubbly chin.

I didn't know how or if I should respond to that comment.

'I have always wanted to be in film. It's my passion. I love stories.'

Frank snorted and I felt my cheeks go red. I was a grown woman of thirty yet in his presence I felt like a child.

'Let me tell you a bit about our vision.' Monica finally put her tablet down and addressed me face to face. 'Are you familiar with R.J. Hellman?'

An instant feeling of panic washed over me as I racked my brain trying to place the name.

'He's a little-known graphic novelist,' she continued, unwittingly alleviating my fear. 'His book, *Water Warriors*, has come to Frank's attention and this is the project we are talking about.'

I had never heard of R.J. Hellman let alone a book called *Water Warriors* but I thought it best to keep my mouth closed and let them do the talking.

'*Water Warriors* is a graphic novel about an alien race that lives under the water. Up on the land people have no idea of their existence. Then one day the Water Race is discovered. It really is a wonderful, imaginative story that will translate beautifully to the big screen.'

I nodded, making a mental note to go and get a copy of this bizarre-sounding book as soon as I'd left the office.

'We are going to shoot it all underwater,' Frank interrupted. 'On a submarine. The film is going to be unlike anything anyone has ever seen. No one has attempted to make an underwater film before. I am going to change that.' He folded his arms across his chest and slightly cocked his head to one side, still examining me. I bit my tongue and decided not to mention *Das Boot*.

'I need an assistant director who will do exactly as I say, no questions asked. I don't want your opinion or your artistic input. I want a skivvy with a good eye.'

'Excuse me'—I adjusted the collar on my shirt as I spoke— 'but why, as you say, use someone with no experience for such a ground-breaking film? I'm sorry, but I don't understand.'

A look crossed his face and I felt Monica tense for a second.

'This film is going to be shot entirely underwater in a submarine. It is going to take months of careful planning and I don't want anyone interfering with my artistic ideas about the project. I need a yes-man'—he paused and small smile crossed his face—'or rather, a yes-woman, by my side.'

'I see,' I said, not fully understanding.

Frank and Monica looked at each other for a moment, then a long silence followed.

'I would love the opportunity to work on this project.' I was desperate to fill the quiet.

'You and every other graduate on the planet,' Frank spat.

Then there was another uncomfortable silence.

'Right!' Monica clapped her hands together once and stood up. 'Thank you for coming, Ms Golding. We will be in touch.'

And just like that the interview was over.

I left the office feeling none the wiser as to what the film was about, let alone why I had been called in, or if the meeting had gone well. All I knew for certain was that I was pleased to get away from the building and away from Frank Holden.

As I walked through Soho, on my way towards the Tube station, I tried to make sense of the strange manner in which the interview had been conducted.

Certain that I was not in the running for the job, I still wanted to learn more about the graphic novel that had inspired Frank and as I passed *Gosh!*, the comic shop on Berwick Street, I felt compelled to investigate.

Behind the counter stood a young man wearing a Green Lantern T-shirt.

'I'm looking for a copy of *Water Warriors*.' I was surprised when his eyes lit up.

'Yeah, sure. It's over here.' He sprung to life and guided me through the maze of shelves to a section at the back of the shop.

'Pure work of genius, that one.' This kid had clearly read everything in the store. 'One of my favourites. So poignant, you know?'

I didn't have a clue but nodded and smiled, holding a copy of the book, if you could call it that, in my hand.

'Will probably be a collector's item in the near future,' he continued, leading me back to the till. 'I've got a first edition at home.' His enthusiasm was as endearing as it was geeky. 'You've got a special edition there,' he said, scanning the book, 'only a couple of hundred copies were ever made.'

'Cool.' I had never read a graphic novel in my life let alone been into a store that specialised in them.

'Okay. That'll be £22.99.' I removed my purse from my bag and handed over my credit card, before examining the rather thin hardback I held in my hand.

'You want a bag?' he asked.

'No thanks.' I'd save myself five pence.

'The artwork is beautiful, you know. Worth every penny.' The kid responded to my obvious surprise at the price.

'Hope so,' I said slipping the book into my bag and crushing the receipt in the palm of my hand.

'Have a good day,' the kid called out as I turned and left the shop.

When I got back to my flat in Dalston, I kicked off my worn suede boots, flung my jacket over the back of a kitchen chair, made myself a large mug of coffee and went and snuggled down on the sofa with my new purchase.

The kid was right. The drawings were amazing and I soon found myself spellbound by the bizarre story about ocean-dwelling aliens.

Skipping lunch, I read right through to the early evening and only stopped when I heard the sound of Olly's key in the door. I'd been so engrossed in the story that I'd almost forgotten I had a boyfriend.

The Pica Explorer

Day One. Hour 00:30.

'**D**o you think we need to wake the others up and tell them what's happened?' Susie speaks in a half whisper. Until then, I haven't thought about the other people on board, only those in the control room.

'Yes. Good idea. Everyone needs to know,' I agree as Susie fumbles with the cuff of her salmon pink sweater, her skinny fingers picking at the wool.

'Frank is livid,' she mutters. I dismiss her concern and head towards the sleeping quarters.

The submarine is a long metal vessel, separated into a number of sections. At the front is the control room, where Patrick and Fiona, the first mate, are usually found. In the middle are the living quarters, with a store room below, and a bunkroom – with beds built into the side of the sub. Beyond that is the lab and computer room, and another store room. And then there's a second bunk room and right at the back is the engine room. It feels more like a space ship than an ocean vessel.

Frank is seated at the table in the living area, clinging to a mug and staring into it with a determined concentration. He doesn't look up as I pass, followed gingerly by Susie. The blue light casts an eerie glow over everything.

Making my way into the first bunkroom, I am greeted by the sound of gentle snoring. To my left, in one of the high beds, Luke lies sleeping, his arm hanging off the bunk. Below him is Anya, a very respected scientist but someone I've found it hard to connect with. She lies with her back to the rest of the room, huddled up beneath her blanket. The other side of the room is abandoned and the beds lie empty with the bedding pushed back.

Following the sound of voices, Susie and I make our way into the second bunkroom beyond, deciding to leave Luke and Anya asleep and in peace for the moment.

'Seems Ray and the others are awake.' I turn my head over my shoulder and whisper to Susie as Ray's loud and distinctive voice travels through the corridor echoing off the metal walls that surround us.

'Someone sounds angry,' Susie adds as we make our way back to the next compartment.

'I told them,' Frank spits, coming up behind us.

'How does this happen?' Ray barges in and stands with his hands on his slender hips. He is a true thesp.

When Ray had gotten on board I'd recognised him immediately. Of course I knew the names of the actors who were going to be involved in the film but the reality of meeting them didn't dawn on me until we stood face to face. As an avid *EastEnders* fan I was slightly in awe of him. At first.

'This can't be.' Dominique appears, draped over Sam who stands there helpless, his face as white as sea foam.

'There must be some sort of system – radar, sonar. Something!'

'Since when did you become a submarine expert?' I can't contain my disapproval.

'Well, we can't just sit here.' The actor looks down at his perfectly manicured nails and shrugs. For a man in his sixties he really should know better than to behave like a child.

'Someone is going to come looking for us, right?' Sam finally speaks. The rest of us remain silent.

Sam Wilson has starred in a few budget B-movies and some ads. I recognised him from a mattress advert. He was better looking in real life than he was on screen, and on screen he looked pretty good.

'Well, say something,' Ray pleads, looking at me.

'Who? Who is going to come looking?' Dominique's eyes fill with tears. 'This was meant to be my big break. Now it looks like I am stuck in this metal can with a group of strangers.' She dabs at her nose, clearly distressed but equally enjoying the drama.

'Don't be so over the top, darling.' Ray rolls his eyes.

'So what is the plan then?' Sam says.

'I think we need to go and talk to our captain,' Ray says, straightening his back.

'Yes. Good idea,' Dominique agrees, still dabbing her nostril with the back of her sleeve and sniffing.

We all follow Ray to the back of the submarine, where the engine room is located. Ray struggles to open the heavy metal door before finally managing to push his way through.

What greets us is a mass of thick grey metal piping, dials and wheels. Patrick, who is dripping with sweat despite the fact the temperature has already dropped considerably since the power went off, is examining some of the dials.

'What the hell is going on?' Ray barks, making Patrick jump. 'Why have we lost power?'

'There has been a short circuit within the batteries.' Patrick remains inspecting the dials. 'An electrical malfunction of sorts. It isn't clear what caused it yet. The engine and communications systems have both shut down.'

'Well turn them back on then.' Ray points a long finger at the captain.

'If only it were that easy.'

'So are you saying we are stuck here?' a wide-eyed Susie asks.

'The most important thing is that everyone remains calm. We have limited oxygen supply. We need to keep our breathing steady.' Patrick does a good job of avoiding answering the question but his comments fill us all with fear.

'We need to try and avoid a build-up of carbon dioxide,' Fiona adds.

'What would be the result if that happened?' Dominique still clings to Sam's arm like a lost child.

'Suffocation is the number one risk.' Patrick's attempt to sound calm is fooling no one. None of us can speak.

'The oxygen generators are running off the backup power system. We probably have about a week's supply.'

'But you can fix the fault affecting the batteries, right?' Sam puts his arm around a blubbering Dominique.

'I don't know.' Patrick looks over at Fiona who remains extremely quiet.

'Do you have scuba gear? Could we just swim out?'

'Are you serious?' Ray smirks.

'Why not?' I stare at him blankly.

Patrick explains gently, 'That is not going to be possible. We are probably two hundred metres below the surface and we don't have the equipment anyway. There is no possible way we would be able open the door.'

'Okay. So you fix the fault and then we get this vessel going again.'

'I will do my best but…' Patrick's words tail off.

'Your best better be good enough,' Ray hisses before marching out of the engine room with his nose in the air.

'I think we need everyone to gather in the living area. We need to talk about this calmly.' Fiona puts her arm on Patrick's shoulder. 'Zara, go and get Frank and Ray and let's all talk this through. We must pull together.'

I nod and leave the engine room, noticing how deafening the silence is. When I get into the living area I find Ray slumped, sitting in one of the chairs with his head in his hands.

'I can't die. Not like this.'

'We don't need to talk about dying. Everything is going to be fine. We just have to stay calm and positive.' I give him my best reassuring smile before leaving the room and going to knock on the bathroom door.

'I'm having a shit!' Frank shouts back in response.

'We are all going to have a talk. Come and join us when you are ready,' I snarl back, the ugly image of Frank sitting on the toilet now ingrained into my psyche.

It is the first time since we sank that I have been alone, and I allow myself a moment to let the magnitude of our situation really sink in. My hands start to shake and I feel my throat closing up. I close my eyes and rest my head against the cold metal wall, knowing that only a few inches away is an entire ocean of water. Then, without any warning, I start to gag before being violently sick.

The smell of it hits my nostrils immediately and I long to be able to open a window.

Moments later Frank arrives, still doing up his flies.

'Clean that shit up,' he says stepping over the puddle of vomit. 'It stinks in here.' He waves a hand under his nose.

My misery mixes with shame.

'Yes, Frank.' I stand up straight again, still tasting the sick in my mouth.

'Disgusting,' I hear him mutter as he heads towards the living area.

Ray

Everyone knew who Frank was. You'd have to have lived in a cave not to, so when I got the call from my agent telling me that he was making a ground-breaking new film, and his casting director had specifically asked for me, I calmly replied that I would attend the audition.

There was a lot of cloak-and-dagger around the film and I was told practically nothing about the role when I agreed to go to the audition. Unfortunately, I was disappointed to learn that Frank would not be present. Instead, a young German casting director was there to put me through my paces.

I'd been acting for nearly forty years and had often had television roles in dramas. For some reason unknown to me, I was often cast as the snotty villain. I was best known for my brief appearance in *EastEnders* as the silver-haired fox who was determined to bring the Mitchell family down. Like many characters before me, I was set up to fail, but working alongside some of those stars was one of my proudest moments and, it goes without saying, meant that my face was often recognised by people on the street.

Fame isn't as glamorous as it may appear. I couldn't step out of my flat without someone shouting my character's name at me or asking for my signature. Oh, and the selfies, the hundreds of selfies I had to pose for grew tedious very quickly. I don't really like people, you see.

Naturally, people wanted to be associated with me due to my fame and success and I will openly admit I used it to my benefit. Getting laid became a doddle. Young men would throw themselves at me and who was I to resist? For a while it was a delicious time. But then the work dried up and I was forgotten. I worked in theatre from time to time, starring in bad whodunnits. It put food on the table but I wasn't happy and felt the success slipping away.

I am classically trained and went to RADA. As a young boy I knew I wanted to act. My father was never around but Mummy would take me to auditions. She had had ambitions of being an actress but had fallen pregnant with me when she was only twenty. In those days most women were expected to stay at home and look after their children. Poor Mummy never stood a chance. Instead she channelled all her motivation into me, her only child.

When she found me playing dress-up in her clothes, rather than chastise me, she encouraged it. 'The boy is just play-acting,' she would say, 'practising his art.' I don't think she understood that I was gay and, even later on when I was grown up, we never discussed my sexuality. I was terrified of disappointing her. She was a strong, overbearing woman.

The audition for the film took place in a small studio in Shoreditch. There was the casting director, a cameraman and me. That was it.

I'd imagined, with Frank's name attached to the production, that there would be a vast budget behind the film. It turned out I was wrong. Still, on the plus side, the German casting director, Jürgen, was a real dish.

'Hello. Ray Neil.' I offered the Aryan looker my most elegant handshake.

'Yes. Take a seat.' He gestured to a chair that was positioned in the middle of the room with a camera and lights pointing at it.

I did as was instructed and sat, crossing one of my long, slim legs over the other.

'Nice jacket,' the German said, not looking up from his notes.

I ran my hand down the burgundy velvet and allowed myself a smile.

'I have them made for me by Edward Sexton on Beauchamp Place.'

Neither Jürgen nor the cameraman responded or looked impressed, which was somewhat disappointing.

'So what exactly is this film about? I've not been given a brief.'

'You will know what you need to know when the time is right.' Jürgen's blue eyes looked at me through his trendy glasses and gave nothing away.

'Ooh, it's all very cloak-and-dagger, isn't it?' I teased.

'Mr Holden wants to keep the details under wraps for now,' the cameraman chipped in, 'so I understand.' His concentration remained on getting his camera in focus.

'That's fine, I suppose, but how can I audition when I have no knowledge of the character I might be playing? This is most unusual.' I did not like being treated like an idiot. 'I have my dignity and as an actor you are asking the impossible of me.' I straightened in the hard plastic chair, knowing that although I wanted to flounce out my credit card bill would not allow me that luxury.

'We need you to be a scientist guy.' Jürgen cleared his throat, put his notes down and folded his arms across his chest.

'What kind of scientist?'

'One who works on a submarine.'

'Oh.' I pondered for a moment, wondering what on earth the film was going to be about.

'You can start to read when you are ready.' Jürgen leant over and handed me a script. 'I will read the other part.' Despite his cold demeanour his smooth German accent held a certain authority and I felt compelled to obey.

'Action.' Jürgen clicked his fingers and pointed at me.

'We are going deeper than any other vessel like this has gone before.' I started reading, trying to find my stride, having had little time to prepare.

'How deep?' Jürgen responded with no emotion or attempt at acting.

This was going to be painful.

***

After a gruelling audition the cameraman was instructed to stop filming and Jürgen announced that it was a wrap.

He tidied the script and notes that lay on the desk in front of him, filed them away into a smart brown leather bag and left the room calling over his shoulder, 'Someone will be in touch', leaving the cameraman and me alone in the room.

We looked at each other, neither really understanding what had just taken place.

'Well, that was odd,' I smirked, trying to disguise my discomfort.

'Never worked like that before.' The young bearded man began to pack up and for the first time since entering the room I was able to get a proper look at him. Until then his face had been hidden behind the large camera on its tripod.

'Have you been in this business for long?' I looked at his buttocks as he bent down to unscrew the camera lens. *Nice*, I thought to myself.

'Been filming for about three years. Do odd jobs here and there but nothing big like this.'

'Are you one of the privileged few who knows what this is all about?' I stood from my chair, my bottom sore from having sat on the hard plastic for so long.

'Nah, not me, mate. I'm just a skivvy.' The young man winked.

'I don't suppose you fancy a drink? There is a quaint little pub just around the corner.' I checked my watch wondering how long I had been in the room.

'Sure. I could do with a pint.'

'I'm sorry, I didn't catch your name...' I extended my hand and we shook.

'Luke.'

'Lovely to make your acquaintance.' His handshake was firm. I liked that.

'Let's get out of here and have a drink. I think we both deserve one after that ordeal.'

'Strange, wasn't it,' Luke agreed. 'Give me five to finish packing up and then I'm all yours.'

I liked the sound of that too and smiled before perching on the desk to wait for him, struggling to keep my eyes off of his arse.

Half an hour later the two of us were in *The Ten Bells* on Commercial Street.

'I love this place. You can sense the history, don't you think?' I sat opposite Luke in the upstairs bar of the pub. Only one other table was occupied. It had just gone five o'clock in the afternoon and the post-work drinkers would soon be descending on us.

Sipping my gin and tonic, I watched Luke glug his beer in earnest.

'Are you London born and bred?'

'Nah, I was brought up in the country. Moved down here for work.'

'How old are you, may I ask?' I inquired, leaning in.

'Twenty-five.' He wiped the froth from his trendy beard and looked around at the chipped tiles on the walls, the peeling wallpaper and candles. 'Bit gothic, isn't it?'

'It has a chequered history.' I smiled to myself. 'Two of Jack the Ripper's victims were associated with the place.'

'Bit grim.' Luke sank more of his beer.

'Fascinating, though, don't you think?'

Luke shrugged and finished his drink.

'Another?'

'Sure, why not,' he agreed as I picked up his empty glass before going over to the bar to order him another pint of ale.

As it just so happened he was sitting with his back to me. I asked the moody-looking barman for another ale. While he prepared the drink I had just enough time to remove the liquid diazepam from the small bottle in my jacket pocket. After the pint was placed on the bar I handed over a crisp ten-pound note. While the barman fetched my change I slipped the liquid into Luke's pint. The dark ale concealed the drug and I lingered for a moment hoping that it would disperse into the ale. Dipping my finger into the liquid I give it a quick stir to encourage it to mix properly.

'Thanks.' Luke accepted the second pint I had bought for him and began to drink.

That is the thing about young men: they will always accept free drinks, even if it means having to spend time with an old poof like me.

By seven o'clock the bar was brimming with revellers and Luke had drunk a skinful. I was careful not to get too drunk and had been ordering simple tonic water, unbeknown to my companion. His eyes looked glazed and he sat slumped in his chair muttering. I could not hear what he was saying because of the noise in the room but every now and then I smiled and nodded, pretending to listen.

An hour later and he was well and truly out of it. I slipped my arm around his torso and guided him out of the pub. He was wobbly on his feet and his head rolled around. No one paid any attention to us as we exited onto the busy street.

We walked for ten minutes, and he began to get heavy. Still, his feet moved along the pavement not know where we were going.

'You've had a bit too much haven't you, you naughty boy.' I allowed my hand to rest on his bum.

'Juss…' His speech was slurred and indecipherable as we wandered along Brick Lane towards the hotel I had in mind.

Above a curry house was the *Brick Lane Hotel*, a one-star establishment that had simple rooms. All I needed was a bed so why break the bank?

We made our way into reception and I had to stop Luke from falling over the threshold.

Moments later I had paid for one night's stay and we made our way towards the room. Luke was beginning to get very heavy, so after I managed to manoeuvre the key into the door I dropped him onto the bed with a thump. He lay on his back, still conscious, just.

After removing my jacket I hung it on the back of the cheap, dated chair and I stood over him for a while, enjoy my moment of power.

***

Half an hour later I was finished and I left Luke sleeping on the bed, snoring like a pig, with his trousers pulled down to his ankles.

'Good night, sweet prince,' I said as I pulled my jacket back on and approached the door, 'I had fun.'

Then I left and slipped away into the night, smiling and knowing that he wouldn't remember a thing.

Child

For what seemed like an age I sat in the cold dark cellar, on the damp floor, next to my bundled up, stained sheets.

The scent of stale air, and my wee, clung to my pyjamas and my skin. I wanted to climb the staircase and bang on the door but I knew Mummy wouldn't let me out. Not until she had calmed down or convinced herself that I had suffered enough.

I'd been down there so many times I felt like I knew each of the spiders personally. I used to be scared of them, especially when the cobwebs would catch on my clothes, but I got used to them. There was one large spindly one that lived in one of the beams. It came out from time to time and rearranged its web. I called it Simon. I thought it was a boy but I couldn't be sure.

I was always a bit surprised how quickly my eyes adjusted to the dark. It only took a few minutes before I could see everything in the cellar. The light from the gap under the door helped, probably.

The thing that was worst of all was that my pyjama bottoms were still wet and clinging to me. I wanted to take them off but then my bottom would be naked against the stone floor, which was so cold.

I hugged myself and rocked backwards and forwards, trying to get warm. A song came into my head and I started singing to myself.

'Hush, little baby, don't say a word...' My voice was dry and crackly. I didn't sound like me.

Then, out of the corner of my eye, I spotted something moving in the far corner and heard a rustling noise.

I stood up. My legs felt wobbly and I backed away until I was up against a wall and couldn't go any further. My eyes strained in the darkness to see what was moving on the other side of the cellar. Then I

26

saw a flash of a pink tail and I knew that there was a rat in the room. I heard it moving around looking for something to eat.

I don't like rats now and I didn't like rats then. They have sharp teeth.

Lying up against the wall was an old broom and I picked it up for protection. I didn't want that creature coming anywhere near me. It might have bitten my toes and I didn't like blood. It has a funny smell. I didn't want my toes to bleed so I stood shaking and holding the broom, keeping my eyes peeled.

Just then, I heard the key being turned in the lock and I dropped the broom, breathing a sigh of relief. As I started to climb the stairs I saw Mummy at the top holding a large bucket.

'This is what you get for being so disgusting!' she yelled as she threw icy water all over me, making me slip on the stairs and lose my footing. Seconds later my chin connected with one of the steps and the door slammed shut again.

The Pica Explorer

Day one. Hour 01:00.

'So what is the plan?' Frank stands at the table with his big arms folded across his broad, puffed up chest while the rest of us sit.

'I can tell you what we know for sure,' Patrick speaks at last. 'There has been a short circuit in the batteries. It's not clear what caused it. The vessel is now probably sitting at a depth of two hundred metres on the ocean floor, somewhere between Norway and the Shetland Islands. We have plenty of food but the issue we face is running out of oxygen. The sub, thankfully, is equipped with military-grade oxygen generators so we probably have up to seven days of breathable air.'

We remain sitting in silence for some time.

'I thought that submarines could stay underwater for months at a time?' Frank finally says something.

'Nuclear vessels, yes. But this is not a nuclear submarine.'

'Okay. But people know we are down here. They will be looking for us. They will send help,' Luke cuts in, looking tired and wiping the sleep from his eyes.

'It isn't as simple as that.' Fiona stands up with a sigh. 'Submarines are built to be stealthy. Even commercial ships such as this. We are currently resting on the seabed and the engines are not working so therefore we are silent. There is no noise coming from the engine, which makes it very difficult for anyone to locate us.'

'That sounds bad.' Dominique's bottom lip begins to quiver.

'It is.' Patrick sounds grave.

'Isn't there any way to get the engine going again? Some way to get this fucking thing back to the surface?'

'There is something we can try but it needs to be discussed first.'

'Well, what the hell is it?' Frank shouts, scowling at Patrick. 'Do it. Whatever it is just get on and bloody do something.'

'It is to do with the floatation. When the sub is working, in order for it to travel deeper, there is a chamber that allows water in, making the vessel heavier so it can descend. In order for the sub to then return to the surface, that chamber needs to be emptied and then filled with air so that it can float.'

'So what are you waiting for?' Sam's voice is high-pitched and full of panic.

'There is a risk that the sub could tip over if we empty the chamber.' Fiona speaks very matter-of-factly but can't disguise the horror plastered across her face. 'Then we could end up damaging the walls of the sub. Worst case scenario, we could spring a leak.'

'That doesn't sound great.' Sam swallows hard.

'No, it fucking doesn't!' Frank roars, slamming his fists down onto the laminate table surface. 'How the hell did this happen? I demand an answer!'

Patrick and Fiona just stare at each other. No one moves.

'Getting arsey isn't going to help here,' Ray says meekly. 'This isn't anyone's fault. Is it?' He turns to Patrick and Fiona, hoping for an answer. Both shake their heads.

'Does the radio work? If not, can it be fixed?' I can feel my hands still shaking and my stomach turning around.

'Is it just me or is it getting colder in here?' Anya says, wrapping her arms tightly around herself.

'Without the power on fully the temperature will drop rapidly,' Fiona admits, sitting down and putting her head in her hands.

'We should all go and put extra clothes on.' Susie offers up an idea.

'Yes, good idea.' Luke stands up and heads towards the sleeping quarters followed by Ray.

'We have some candles. They will help with light and heat,' Patrick says, trying to remain positive.

'I'll fetch them.' Fiona gathers herself together again and sets off towards the back of the sub.

'Are we going to freeze to death?' Dominique is as pale as a ghost and her large green eyes look searchingly at Patrick.

'No, that won't happen. But we do all need to calm down and try and preserve the oxygen supply.'

'What good is that if no one will ever rescue us?' Sam spits, finally finding his backbone.

It is at this point that Frank storms out of the living area towards the control room. 'I need some fucking peace,' he shouts while stomping away. 'I suggest all of you leave me alone.'

'Should someone go after him?' Susie looks like a deer caught in the headlights. Her thin slender neck supports a delicate head that is slightly cocked.

'Leave him to it,' Anya says, unfazed. 'He needs time to calm down.'

Moments later Fiona returns with a supply of candles. 'Here we are,' she says, setting them up around the living area, 'we must remember to blow them out when we go to sleep.'

'Sleep?' I turn to her in amazement. 'Do you really think any of us are going to get any sleep?'

'We need to conserve our energy and rest. We must think clearly.'

'You're on another fucking planet, darling!' The look of disdain on Sam's face makes him ugly for a moment.

'Can everyone please stop fighting,' Susie begs, putting her hands up over her ears like a child. Anya, sensing the rising tension, puts her arm around Susie and guides her towards the kitchen.

I am left standing with Dominique and Sam, neither of whom have anything to say. The real weight of the situation has now settled on each and every one of us.

'We aren't getting out of this alive.' I slump down on the floor and let the wave of nausea course through me.

As I close my eyes I hear Sam and Dominique whisper to one another before footsteps fade, leaving me alone in the living area.

Patrick

'Ever since I was small I've had an interest in science. As a boy I would collect bugs and study them. Then, when I was older, my parents took me to the seaside and I fell in love with the ocean.

I remember that trip to Weston-super-Mare like it was yesterday. We went during the Easter holidays. The sky was grey and the sea was angry. Big waves came crashing down onto the sand, pulling it back with watery claws and throwing it up again. I knew then that I wanted to live on the coast and when I went to university to study physics I did just that.

Southampton was a world away from where I grew up in Derbyshire. I'd lived in the countryside, in a small village called Over Haddon near Bakewell for most of my life, and the city was a new experience for me.

My parents were extremely proud when my teacher told them I was university material and they worked very hard to make sure I could attend and follow my ambition.

At Southampton I kept my head down, still daunted by the size and pace of the city, and concentrated on my work. But that changed when I met Anita. She was a coy young woman who was also far from home. She was a Yorkshire lass studying at the university just like me.

It was the seventies and I had long hair and bad clothes. I still have the long hair; although it is less brown now and more salt and pepper.

I spotted Anita one afternoon in the library, head buried in a book. She was pale with pink cheeks and sparkling blue eyes. Pretty and understated in her looks, she was the sort of woman that I fancied immediately.

In those days, I hadn't had much experience with women but she seemed approachable and had an open face so I plucked up the courage to talk to her. When I did, her cheeks flushed a darker shade of pink and I found it endearing.

I introduced myself and asked her if I might sit down at her table. She smiled and indicated to a chair. We got talking, and I asked her how long she'd been in Southampton and what she was studying. Anita told me about her life growing up just outside of Sheffield and explained that she was an English student. I could have listened to her soft Yorkshire accent for hours, and did so. We talked for so long that the stuffy old woman who was in charge of the library had to ask us to leave as it was closing. We gathered our books and shuffled out giggling. Then we went and had a pizza. That was our first date.

Two years later we were married and living in a damp basement flat in the centre of the city. We were broke and still studying but it didn't matter; we were happy.

She graduated a year before me and had dreams of becoming a writer, but fate played its hand and she discovered she was pregnant before she had a chance to start her novel. I worked all the hours I could to make ends meet while trying to juggle my studies.

Finally we had enough money to move out of the dingy basement flat and moved further out of town to a small two-up two-down. Anita spent time doing the place up and making it a home suitable for the three of us. She did an especially fine job on the nursery, making sure that it was a nice neutral yellow, since we didn't know the sex of the unborn child.

In March 1977 Anita gave birth to our daughter, Rosie. She was a plump little thing with a broad round face. I couldn't see myself in her, but she was the spitting image of her mother.

Later that same year I graduated with a first. That is when we began to fight. I wanted to go on to do a master's but Anita wanted me to get a job and start providing more for our family. I told her it had been my dream to be a scientist and she said that dreams were for losers and that I had responsibility now.

Despite her disapproval, after working in a dead-end job for a year, I went back to university to do a master's in physics and I was happy once again. But very soon after I started the course Anita announced she was pregnant for a second time. We had discussed putting off having another baby until after I'd finished at Southampton, but Anita told me that her contraceptive pill must have failed. I still don't believe her to this day.

Eight months later my son, Richard, was born, named after my father. He was a serious little boy and very different from his sister. It seemed Anita and I had reproduced ourselves more or less exactly. Anita was busy with the children and I threw myself into my work. It didn't take long for us to grow apart.

I'd known soon after Rosie was born that Anita longed to move back to Yorkshire, but I wasn't ready to swap life in the city and my education for a quiet life in the country. I wanted more than that. I wanted to be a pioneer in my field but she didn't understand where I was coming from. Motherhood changed her.

I found myself spending more and more time at college, working late in the library and in the science block. I'd come home late to find her asleep on the sofa and my dinner, cold, on the table. But I didn't have the desire to wake her up and talk to her so I would take myself upstairs to bed. It turns out that I wasn't cut out to be a husband and soon we became no more than two people sharing a house.

Life became more complicated when I met Julie. She was five years my junior and an undergraduate at the university. Our paths first crossed when she appeared in one of the labs, there working on a project of her own.

The chemistry was instant and the affair began that night. She was so different to the woman Anita had become. She was sexy and ballsy. She made me laugh.

Julie didn't care that I was married. She enjoyed the thrill of it all. We weren't in love, it was just sex, but that didn't make Anita feel any better when she discovered the affair. That week she packed her bags, and left to go back to Yorkshire to live with her parents, taking the children with her.

Rosie and Richard grew up never really knowing me. I went to visit once in a while but their mother had it in for me and poisoned their young minds. I don't blame her, really, but it has always been a regret that I was a let-down as a father.

When Anita left, Julie dumped me. She'd met another student on her course who she started a relationship with. I was less heartbroken and more irritated by the whole thing at the time.

The small house felt empty without the children and Anita so I moved back into the centre and rented a bedsit, determined to concentrate on my studies and remain celibate in the meantime.

In eighty-two, I finished my master's and went on to start my PhD at Durham, before becoming an engineer on board a submarine, which is where I learnt how to pilot one.

I was happy in Durham, although it was smaller than Southampton and had less going on. It gave me the shove I needed to throw everything I had into my paper. Four years later I left Durham as Dr Skuse. It was one of the proudest moments of my life.

Being a red-blooded male, I had my share of girlfriends during my time there. I was, for some reason, popular with women who liked my relaxed approach and were impressed by my mind. But none of them made me want to settle down. I was more in love with my work than I could ever be with a woman.

For nearly two decades I spent time doing research, thanks to government grants, before returning to education, this time as an engineering lecturer. In certain circles my name meant something so, when I decided to investigate the possibility of lecturing, the offers came in thick and fast. I returned to Southampton for a while and taught there, but the place had changed and I no longer recognised the city I'd spent time in. Soon I put in a request for a transfer and ended up in Plymouth, where I was happy.

But I've always had a nomadic personality and despite the fun I had with some of the young female students, I got bored with being in one place and I missed being at sea. So, I put the feelers out and it didn't take long before I heard about an opportunity on board The Pica Explorer.

Still, I couldn't quite leave all my habits behind, so when I was offered the position as captain on the research vessel I offered a job to a sweet young thing I'd become fond of while teaching in Plymouth. In some ways, she reminded me of Anita and I thought I had been given an opportunity to right a wrong. Having grown older and wiser I realised how badly I'd let both my children and my ex-wife down.

I'd never fancied Anya, but she was bright and keen. She was more than willing to join me on my new adventure and I liked the idea of having someone familiar around.

The research mission, which lasted three months, was a success and I worked well alongside Anya and the rest of the crew. It was good being back at sea and I realised how much I'd missed it.

Upon returning to land I was given the chance to return to sea again to do research on shark species in the North Sea. Sadly, my co-captain was due to get married and was unable to join us on that expedition. So I set about looking for a replacement and came across Fiona, who fit the bill perfectly.

Fiona and I shared a passion for the ocean and soon developed a desire for one another. She was feisty and strong, and the start of our affair was extremely exciting, made more so by the fact that she was twenty-five years my junior. Life was good but was about to take an interesting turn. Never had I expected to receive a call telling me that The Pica Explorer was going to be used in the making of a film. It was the most surreal moment of my career. Of course, I had heard of Frank Holden. In my time I had watched plenty of films, and the prospect of getting to meet and work alongside such an industry giant filled me with excitement. This would be a very different type of adventure and I welcomed it.

We were told very little about the film – just that it was set on a submersible craft and that a small crew of filmmakers and actors would be on board with us. I had to sign a disclaimer promising never to discuss what happened during filming or to discuss the story or process with anyone, which I was more than happy to do.

To my bitter disappointment, the moment Frank Holden stepped on board I took a dislike to him. He was brash, arrogant and rude, which meant, sadly, that I could not look forward to the next few weeks spent in his company.

The Pica Explorer

Day two. Hour 08:00.

I'm sitting in the living area alone. Some of them have managed to go to sleep while Patrick and Fiona remain in the engine room problem-solving, although they both clearly think it is hopeless.

Frank is sitting at the front of the sub, in the control seat, just staring out into the dark water that surrounds us. I went in earlier to check if he was okay but the scowl on his face told me it was best I leave him alone.

One lonely candle is burning. We are saving the others. I watch as the level of wax slowly creeps down, like sand in an egg timer, taunting me.

Out of nowhere I hear a blood-curdling scream coming from the back of the sub. I rush towards the noise, my heart thumping in my chest, feeling like it might erupt. The back of the sub is dark now and I feel my way through the corridor towards the bunkroom. The screaming hasn't abated.

As I make it through the doorway a flashlight comes on.

'Why the fuck are you making all that noise?' Sam is holding the torch shakily and I doubt he managed to get any sleep.

In the spotlight stands Dominique as pale as a ghost. Her whole body is shaking and silent tears are streaming down her white face.

'What is it?' Sam asks again, this time more gently.

My heart is in my throat and I can hear the blood pumping in my ears as her long quivering finger points to one of the beds.

Lying quite still on his back, looking skywards, is Ray. His eyes are rolled back and his mouth is hanging open like a fish. From his neck protrudes a syringe.

Anya, who is now fully out of her bunkbed, follows the light and dashes towards the corpse to search for signs of life. She checks his pulse on both his wrist and his neck but it is pointless. He is dead.

'What the hell is all the noise about?' Frank comes storming in with a face like thunder. When he sees Ray's body he is silenced.

'Who? What?' Sam stares in horror at the lifeless body.

'Rigor mortis is beginning to set in,' Anya says. 'He must have been dead for at least two hours. What the hell is going on round here?' She looks really shaken.

'How do you know?' Susie has appeared.

'I'm a scientist. We know these things.' She shrugs.

'Everyone out of here,' Frank orders, looking less confident than usual.

'Why?' Anya asks.

'Because this is a crime scene and there is a fucking dead man lying on a bed,' he growls.

'Who are you, Hercule fucking Poirot?' Sam smirks to himself.

'Get the fuck out of this room right now before I lay one on you.' Frank approaches Sam. He is a tall man and towers above the young actor.

'Okay.' Sam accepts meekly and takes Dominique by the hand, leading her out of the way.

'What do you mean "a crime scene"?' I ask.

'Well, he didn't put the fucking needle in his own larynx did he!' Frank gestures towards Ray.

Just then we all stop. No one moves. No one says a word.

'You mean he was killed?' Susie's voice shakes.

'Well done, genius,' Frank says, pushing her out of the way and leaving the rest of us standing looking at the body.

'Oh my God,' Dominique says as her legs begin to go. Thankfully Sam is there to catch her and Anya jumps up to assist him.

'Let's take her through into the living room. Come on, everyone. I think Frank is right. Let's leave the room.' The rest of us follow Anya and Sam who are both supporting Dominique.

In the corridor Patrick and Fiona meet us.

'What's happened?' The exhaustion on Fiona's face is apparent.

'Ray... I... he's dead.'

'What!' Patrick's voice rises.

'Come into the living area. We're all going in there.'

'Yes, follow us,' Anya calls from the front.

Fiona and Patrick share a startled look before agreeing to join us in another part of the vessel.

When we reach the living area we find Frank sitting at the table glaring at us all. His little brown eyes are shining as if they are dancing with fire.

'What have we done?' Sam whines.

'One of you has killed a man,' Frank growls.

'Oh, this is ludicrous!' Sam protests fervently.

'What is going on here?' Patrick's voice is quiet but authoritative. 'I demand to know. I am still the captain on board this vessel.'

'Someone killed Ray,' Frank says calmly.

'Killed him?' Fiona gasps while Anya and Sam manage to position Dominique so that she is sitting down. She is barely conscious.

'Dead as a dodo.' Frank's choice of words is far from appropriate.

I look over at Luke who hasn't spoken since we discovered Ray's body. He has a strange look on his face.

'Are you okay, Luke?' He has dark circles around his eyes and his cheeks, which are normally full of colour, look gaunt.

'Not really. This is fucking nuts.' He scratches his beard and I notice that his body is shaking slightly. As is mine.

'I need a drink.' Frank gets up, pushing his large gut past Patrick, and opens a cupboard. 'Anyone else?' He holds up a bottle of Scotch.

'I will,' I say. I'm the only one to take him up on his offer and I have a moment of guilt for siding with Frank.

Frank pours two large glasses of Scotch and hands me one.

'Get that down you, doll.' He clinks my glass and then takes a large swig of his drink, holding it for a moment in his cheeks before swallowing.

The whisky is harsh and warm on my throat but feels good as it hits my stomach. Olly loves whisky and I realise how much I miss him.

'Who was it then?' Anya asks as if addressing a classroom, breaking my train of thought.

'Who was what?' Susie looks at her puzzled.

'Who killed the actor?' Anya replies coldly.

'Yes, I'd like to know which one of you fuckers killed one of my leading men.' Frank glares at us each in turn.

No one says a word.

'Patrick and I have been together in the engine room the whole time,' Fiona says defensively.

'It's true,' Patrick agrees. 'Besides, neither of us had met him until he set foot on my sub.'

'So you say,' Frank mutters under his breath.

'This is ridiculous. No one killed him. He must have done it to himself.' Sam shrugs. 'Probably freaked the fuck out about our situation and decided suicide was the only option.'

'Don't be stupid,' Anya hisses.

'Okay, come on, calm down everyone.' Susie clearly does not like tension.

'Where did the syringe come from? That's what I want to know.' Frank drains the last of his drink.

'I believe it came from the first aid kit we keep on board,' Anya confesses.

'Where is that normally kept?' I ask.

'On a wall between the bunkrooms and the engine room. Everyone had access to it.'

'I'm going to check it now,' Patrick says marching out of the living room leaving the eight of us in silence.

We start to look at each other, wondering if there really is a killer among us and, if so, who it is.

Moments later Patrick returns with a grave expression on his face.

'The adrenaline auto injector is missing from the kit.'

'So we now know where it came from but we still don't know who took it,' Luke concludes.

'Why would anyone want to kill Ray, though?' Sam asks. 'None of us really know him, do we? Why would any of us want him dead?'

'A good question,' I say after taking another sip of the whisky.

In turn, I examine the face of each of my companions. Every one looks as perplexed as the next. Some look frightened and others look baffled. Luke hangs his head and refuses to make eye contact.

'Have you all forgotten our other current predicament?' Fiona puts her hands on her hips. She is attractive, in a way, with her curvy figure and shoulder-length dark chocolate bob.

For a moment I had been so distracted by the drama, I'd briefly forgotten we were sitting, trapped, on the bottom of the ocean. As the realisation returns I feel my stomach begin to turn and the whisky threatening to come back up.

'I can't breathe,' I say getting to my feet as the world around me starts to spin. 'I need some air.'

'We all do, doll.' Frank chuckles bitterly.

'Are you okay, Zara?' Susie approaches, her eyes full of concern.

'Not really.' I close my eyes in an attempt to shut everything out.

'Come on. Come with me.' Susie puts her skinny arm around my shoulder.

'Where are we going?' I ask, feeling like I might pass out.

'Anywhere but here.'

Dominique

The audition, as intimidating as it was, went well, in a way. At first, Frank Holden wasn't anything like as scary as I'd imagined. He was authoritative, yes, but a real gentleman. I would have described him as a charmer. At least those were my first impressions.

On that chilly but crisp February morning I got on the Tube and made my way to West London. As instructed by my agent, who up until that point had been worse than useless, I wore a black cocktail dress and heels. It seemed unusual to have a dress code for an audition but I am not long out of stage school and so I always do as I am told.

For as long as I can remember I've been involved in the performing arts. I started out with ballet and progressed quickly through the stages, eventually joining a dance school at the age of thirteen. My parents were keen that I should follow my dreams and make the most of my talents. As I was an only child they sank all their hopes, ambitions and money into me. I was very lucky.

My childhood was easy and comfortable. I went to a good school and lived in a large house with plenty of land, which meant I could have a horse. Butterbelle was a Welsh cob and a beautiful palomino.

I would spend hours with her, grooming her flaxen mane and tail. She was my best friend. Despite the love and energy my parents gave to me I always longed for a sibling. I suppose Butterbelle was the next best thing.

Unfortunately, after becoming extremely ill and suffering with bulimia nervosa, I had to leave dance school, but soon after that decided I would turn my attention to acting instead. I wasn't as natural at it as I had been at ballet but I enjoyed the feeling of being on stage again.

The teachers and my parents kept a careful eye on me, monitoring what I was eating and my weight but, gradually, as I got better they began to relax.

I will never know whether my illness was linked to my desire to succeed as a dancer, but I suspect it probably was. The pressure on dancers to remain thin is heavy.

My mother told me that my beauty would take me a long way in this world and that I could do whatever I desired. So, when I was sixteen, I put myself forward to some modelling agencies and the work quickly started to pour in. I'd never had dreams of being a model but the money was good and I needed to do something to pay the bills while I struggled to make it as an actress. I was determined not to live off my parents' money forever.

In the five years since leaving drama school I've got to know parts of London well and have come to see it as my home, despite being born and bred in the countryside. But London is such a vast place there are still areas of it that remain foreign to me and always will.

After getting off the Tube, I walked along Sloane Street, passing designer shops, expensive restaurants and lovely boutiques. The whole area smelt of money and I looked longingly into shop windows at clothes and jewellery that I could only dream of affording.

To my surprise, when I turned up at Frank Holden's building, I discovered that it wasn't his offices I was visiting but his home. His lavish apartment was situated in Knightsbridge and had an exclusive One Hyde Park building address.

A man wearing a suit opened the main door to the building and I was ushered into the foyer. There, sitting behind a large desk, was a concierge who smiled and asked which apartment I was visiting.

'I'm here to see Frank Holden,' I whispered quietly, feeling self-conscious in my new heels, which were now rubbing and starting to cause blisters.

'Take the lift to level two,' the well-spoken concierge replied, signalling towards the elevator on the left-hand side of the large entrance hall.

Walking slowly, so as to not anger my feet further, I pressed the button for the lift and waited patiently.

Although my acting experience was minimal, I had done lots of modelling and was used to being in front of the camera. My good looks held me back in some ways but they had also led me to that moment, standing there waiting for a lift in Frank Holden's prestigious apartment building, and for that I was grateful.

By the time I'd made it to the second floor my nerves were really beginning to kick in. I'd been given little information about the film I would be auditioning for and felt daunted by meeting the director for the first time at his home. It didn't help that the balls of my feet were aching and the backs of my shoes were cutting through my stockings and into the flesh on my heels.

Taking a deep breath and standing as straight as I could, given my shoe situation, I knocked as confidently as I could manage on the door.

A large-bellied man with thinning hair and small eyes opened the door and looked me up and down. He was older than I had imagined. He was wearing only a dressing gown.

'Dominique.' He lunged forward, slipping his arms around my waist and kissed my cheek as if we were old friends.

Thrown by his overly friendly welcome, I remained standing on the wrong side of the door, not knowing what to do.

'Come in, doll.' He winked and moved back so that I could pass. Stepping into his home was like walking into a world I'd never encountered before. The curved hallway of his opulent apartment was both grand and elegant, modern and light despite the dark wood panelling. I could see at the end of the hallway there was a very large reception area with a large balcony, which I imagined he used to entertain.

As we went into the main living space there was a well-proportioned open-plan kitchen, which led to the living room

that had its own double door entrance. To the right, through a
wide open door, I could see a beautiful double bedroom and a
huge king-size bed made up with dark grey satin sheets.

'You like it?' Frank watched me look on in awe at his
home before clapping his hands together and saying the word
'lights'. Instantly the lights were dimmed, which seemed like an
unnecessary thing to do given that the winter sun was flooding
in anyway.

'Let me take your coat,' he said, slipping his large hands around
my shoulders and removing it for me before I had a chance to
disagree.

'Thank you.' I felt ridiculous standing there in a cocktail dress
on a weekday morning. Particularly given that there only appeared
to be two of us in the apartment.

'Can I get you a drink? Champagne?' He sauntered over to the
marble table and removed a bottle of chilled champagne from a
designer cooler filled with ice.

It was not yet midday but I didn't want to appear rude so
accepted the glass he was already pouring.

'So tell me about yourself, Dominique.' He said my name in
a way that made me feel uncomfortable.

'I've always wanted to be an actress,' I started speaking and he
rolled his eyes.

'No, no, stop.' He put a large hand up. 'I'm not interested in
hearing any old spiel. Tell me something you haven't told anyone
else.'

Standing before me was a renowned filmmaker, who was
wearing only a fluffy white dressing gown, supplying me with
champagne and asking me inappropriate questions. What could
I do? I was terrified of upsetting him, or blowing my chance of
acting in his next film, so I said what I thought he wanted to
hear.

'I once was asked to be in a porn film.' I don't know where
that came from. It wasn't even true but I sensed this was the kind
of thing he was after.

'Please tell me you did it?' His piggy eyes glinted and his fat tongue ran across his lips.

'I err…' The words escaped me.

'Well, missy, if you want to have a part in my next film perhaps you'd better show me what you're made of.'

He went and sat on the sofa and patted the cushion next to him.

'This film is going to require men and women living in very close quarters. I need to know you're up to the…'—he paused grinning—'position.'

He undid his robe and began to massage himself. Horror-struck by the vile act taking place in front of me, I froze. I wish I'd run out screaming but I didn't. I just stood there while he finished himself off.

'Oh you're good.' He wiped his hand on his robe before retying it. 'You're a good girl but a dirty girl.' He smirked, pointing to the ground.

What I hadn't realised until then was that in my shock I'd spilt the contents of my champagne glass onto his plush cream carpet.

'I'm sorry.' My throat felt dry but I was too scared to kneel and clean it up.

'Don't sweat it, doll. I'll call housekeeping and get them to come and deal with it. Benefit of being rich and famous.' He chuckled.

Still I remained glued to the spot wondering if I'd just imagined what had taken place.

'You got the part, kid. I'll get my people to call your agent and give you the details.'

The mixture of horror and elation was not like anything I'd ever felt before.

'Great,' I managed to whisper.

'But, doll, you know how this works, right?' He fixed me with a stare and all of the faked softness left his face. 'You talk to anyone about this and I will make sure you never act again.'

Then his face relaxed once more as he slipped behind me and helped me to put my coat on before pressing up against me. 'Now, be a good girl, keep your mouth shut and fuck off.'

I have never left a building as quickly as I did that day.

It took some time to get through the London crowds and make my way back to the flat that I shared with friends in Fulham. The first thing I did was put all the clothes I had worn that morning in the bin. Then I took a long hot shower.

I cried for a week afterwards, but never dreamt of turning down the part when my agent got in touch and excitedly confirmed that I had been offered a role in the film. Neither did I ever consider telling anyone what took place in Frank's apartment. I would rather have died.

Child

When I started to fail my spelling tests things got worse for me. Mummy was so angry, and so ashamed that her child was thick, she began to punish me much more frequently.

I decided to try and hide the results of my homework from her but when she found out she would get even angrier.

'You're thick,' she'd spit, 'just like your father. Thick and worthless.' Her newfound toy to play with was a thick metal belt. She always used the end that had the buckle. I will never forget the sound it made when it connected with my skin. 'I rid myself of your father because he was useless. Am I going to have to get rid of you too, you little shit?' she would roar before taking me down to the cellar to beat me.

I used to think she took me down there to frighten me, but as I grew older I realised it was because my screams could not be heard so easily.

I'd never known my father. We had never met. Mummy told me that as soon as he discovered she was pregnant he up and left without a word. She said it was my fault that she was on her own.

'If only I'd gone to the clinic when I found out I was carrying you,' she would say, 'I could have had a decent life.' Mummy would rant while she tied my hands to a pipe in the cellar and stripped my torso bare. Then the whipping would begin. She only ever did seven lashes. No more, no less. And with each hit she would recount the seven deadly sins, although I never really understood why.

When she had finished, she would then cover my bruised and battered back with a woollen blanket and leave me down there, still tied to the pipe. I hated that blanket. It smelt like mothballs and on occasion, when the belt buckle would rip my skin, the fibres of wool would cling to the wound as it dried. When she reappeared to untie me, I dreaded having to shed the blanket because I knew it would open up the wounds again.

'I don't know why you make me do this,' she'd mutter, pushing me up the stairs as my wobbly legs did their best to climb each step.

Once at the top, it always took me a while for my eyes to adjust to the light and I'd squint, almost wishing I was back down in the darkness again.

'Sorry, Mummy.'

'Go and wash yourself. You're a mess and you stink.' Then she'd take herself off to the kitchen to pour herself a large vodka, leaving me to clean myself up and tend to my wounds. Every time she beat me with the belt I knew I would not get supper that night and I would go to bed hungry – yet another of her punishments that I had to endure. But as the abuse started to become a routine I worked out ways to avoid feeling hungry.

At school, at lunchtime, I started to sneak fruit out of the lunch hall. I kept it in my sports bag, which Mummy never checked. I would take the fruit home, where I kept it in the bottom of my cupboard, ready for the nights when I knew I wouldn't be fed. It worked for a while and I got away with it but then one day Mummy found out.

I came home from school on a Thursday in December to discover the house was quiet and Mummy was nowhere to be found. She had never not been at home when I'd returned from school before so I knew something was wrong.

Wanting to hide the apple I had in my sports bag, I skipped up the stairs to my bedroom, but when I opened the door I found Mummy sitting on the bed. Next to her was a pile of fruit. She'd found my secret stash.

A cigarette hung from her mouth and she just sat there, arms crossed, staring at me. I came into the room, closed the door and hung my head in shame.

'You think you're clever, don't you? You thought I wouldn't realise you were hiding food. You are so stupid I sometimes struggle to accept you came out of my body.' A large piece of ash fell from her cigarette and onto my bed sheets as she picked up a large red apple and inspected it. A crooked smile spread across her lips and she looked at me from below her eyelashes. Then she stood up and hurled the apple at me.

The fruit hit me in the chest, knocking the wind right out of me. Seconds later she was hurling it all in my direction, one piece at a time. I crouched on the ground and attempted to cover my head as apples rained down on me hard. One hit me in the face and split my eyebrow open. Another hit me on the back where wounds were still attempting to heal.

When she had finished she sat back down on the bed panting. My skull ached and the blood was running down my face blinding me in one eye. It was then that I wet myself in front of her.

The urine bounced off the wooden floorboards making a loud noise, and my shame was complete.

'You disgusting little maggot.' Mummy came over to where I was crouching on the ground and grabbed me by the throat. Her eyes were wide and bloodshot.

'Clean yourself right now,' she bellowed, making sure she didn't stand in the puddle of wee.

Unable to breathe as her grip tightened, I wished right then that I could die.

Then without warning she released me and I collapsed into a heap on the floor, lying in my own urine.

'No Christmas and no dinner,' she said as she left the room, slamming the door closed behind her while I lay shaking and trying to breathe.

It did not take long for the tears to come and that night, as she had promised, I went to bed hungry and in a lot of pain.

The Pica Explorer

Day two. Hour 08:45.

We have decided it would be best if we moved Ray's body into one of the large freezers. It meant having to take a lot of food out, and risk it going off, but that is a better prospect than having a rotting body under our noses.

Thankfully I am not involved in the task of moving him. Patrick, Sam and Luke are doing it, though Sam is making an awful fuss. Frank, meanwhile, has refused to help, leaving the other three men to it.

The rest of us leave the room and also the sound of the men grunting and groaning as they lift Ray's lifeless body.

'Heavy, for a skinny guy,' Luke pants as I walk away, linking arms with Susie.

'They say that a body is heavier when it's dead than when it's alive,' Susie whispers.

'I've heard that too. I wonder why.'

She shrugs and pulls the woollen cardigan back on, which was slipping off her shoulder. 'I'm cold.' She shudders. 'Do you think we can still use the showers? I just want to wash all of this away.'

I hug her. 'I know, me too.'

As we enter the living area again, solemn faces greet us. Every person in the room looks grim. 'We need to eat. We must keep our energy up.' Fiona gets to her feet and rubs her tired eyes. 'Besides, all that food will go off if we don't.'

'Well, I for one am starving.' Frank pats his large gut with pride.

'How can you even think of eating at a time like this?' Susie asks, horror-struck. 'A man has just been killed.'

'We cannot all just give up and die too.' Anya agrees with Fiona but refuses to look her in the eye.

'Very well. I'll prepare something for us all.' Fiona claps her hands together in an efficient manner and leaves the room.

'I could do with some meat,' Frank mutters.

I see Dominique turn quite green and then dash out of the room towards the loo.

'You really are an animal,' Anya spits at Frank with a look of contempt.

'All animal,' Frank growls just as Patrick, Luke and Sam appear. 'But I didn't plunge that needle into Ray's scrawny neck and one of you did. So who here really is the animal?'

'What's going on?' Patrick asks, wiping a bead of sweat from his temple.

'All done?' Susie says quietly.

'Yes.' Patrick nods and looks grave.

'Well, Fiona has gone to make us all something to eat.' Anya stands and moves away from Frank.

'Good.'

I can't hold it in anymore. 'I'm sorry, but has everyone forgotten the fucking predicament we are facing?'

The room goes quiet, so much so that you can hear the flicker of the candle flame. No one says a word.

'Come on, everyone!' My voice is rising in pitch with each word. 'What are we going to do?' Still silence. 'Patrick.' I turn to face him. 'Please, you are the captain; you must know what to do. Surely there is something...' My words trail off when I realise Patrick can't look me in the eye and has instead fixed his stare to a spot on the floor.

'He doesn't have a clue.' Frank bangs his fist on the table in frustration. 'We've been sent down here with a fucking cowboy! And to top it off, one of you fuckers is a killer.'

'No,' Anya interjects as her cheeks grow red, 'don't speak to him like that.'

'It's okay, Anya, really.' Patrick smiles at her gratefully. 'We are all upset.'

'Upset?' Frank chuckles bitterly. 'This is your tin can, but you can't fix it, can you?'

'I can't stand any more of this!' I sink to the floor holding my head in my hands as the claustrophobic world I inhabit starts to spin.

'Get her a glass of water,' I hear Susie say, although her voice sounds far away. 'I think she might faint.'

And just then everything starts to go black and their words slip away until I can hear and see nothing.

The Pica Explorer

Day three. Hour 07:00.

W hen I wake up, I am lying on a bunk in the same room where Ray died. No one else is here and the quiet wraps its hands around my throat as I sit bolt upright trying to breathe.

A glass of water has been placed on my bedside and I drink the cool liquid as if my life depended on it. Once the glass has been drained I put it back down and wipe my lips dry. The room is dark and I feel like a prisoner in this place. The metal, the cold, the strange noises that seem to echo around the whole of the submarine only compound my fear and I wish that I was back on land.

I cannot bring myself to imagine what might be living in the water that surrounds us. At this depth I suspect there are some very strange looking creatures.

Even now, as an adult, I don't like being out of my depth when I'm in the sea. The thought of sharks, eels and jellyfish terrify me. They are so alien. I was stung once by something in the sea off Sicily and it hurt like hell.

I've always thought that I stood more chance of making it back to shore if I didn't go out of my depth. How ironic that I now find myself so far out of my depth and, worse still, that I am going to die down here.

As that thought crosses my mind I find myself starting to feel sick once more and a thin layer of sweat appears instantly across my skin and my mouth fills with bitter-tasting bile.

Somewhere in the distance I can hear voices. The others are talking but their words are muffled and I cannot make out what it is they are saying.

Gingerly, I get up off my bunk, feeling somewhat like Bambi on ice. Steadying myself with my hand, I lean against the cold metal for a moment and close my eyes, hoping the dizziness will pass. Putting my ear to the door I listen to the people speaking on the other side.

'Who do you think it is?' I recognise Dominique's voice.

'Not a clue but I'd bet it is one of the men,' Sam replies.

'Yes, no woman could ever be so brutal.'

'I suspect Frank. He's got a hell of a temper.'

'Maybe.' Dominique sounds distant and I listen to their footsteps trail away.

Just then I hear a scream coming from somewhere in the sub.

Without even realising my legs are managing to move, I find myself seeking the person responsible for the noise as I open the door and trip along the narrow corridor, feeling my way in the near total darkness. As I pass by one of the small round windows something catches my eye and I stop.

Outside, in the cold water, a light from the submarine is shining on something. I peer a little closer and realise that the something is a large, grotesque shark. In horror I recoil backwards, banging my head on a thick pipe. The large, cumbersome creature appears to have stopped by the window to look inside. Its small, milky, soulless eye stares in through the minute window.

It is super-sized and must be at least six metres long. Perhaps everything in the depths is bigger.

I know it cannot get to me but the fact that we are trapped in its territory, unable to escape, fills me with dread. The creature remains quite still, floating next to the sub. It opens its large jaws and now it is my turn to scream.

Moments later, Sam, Luke and Dominique appear to investigate.

'Are you all right?' Luke asks looking ashen.

Unable to speak I point at the prehistoric fish with a quivering hand.

'Oh, that's cool.' Luke moves closer to get a better look while Dominique comes over to me and puts her long slender arm around me.

'It can't hurt you,' she soothes.

'What is all the noise?' Anya has appeared and stands looking unimpressed with her hands on her hips.

'She freaked because of the shark.' Luke nods his head towards the direction of the window as Anya steps forward, pushing him out the way so that she can see.

'It is a Greenland shark,' she says, as if that should mean something to any of us. We all stare at her blankly.

'It is one of the largest species in the ocean. It is a scavenger shark that is drawn to the smell of rotting flesh.'

'Lovely,' Sam adds, wrinkling up his nose.

'It knows,' I manage to stutter. 'Somehow it knows.'

'Knows what?' Anya turns to me and rolls her eyes.

'That we are all going to die here. It can smell our fear.'

Dominique starts to stroke my head. 'No, sweetie. It doesn't.'

'Then why is it staring at us?'

'It has probably just come to investigate the sub.' Anya shrugs. 'Anyway, enough of this, you scared me half to death. Please don't scream like that. Our nerves are all on tenterhooks as it is.'

And then I remember.

'I wasn't me,' I say. 'I mean, it was me but it wasn't just me. I heard someone else cry out too. That's why I'm here. I came to see what the screaming was about. I think it came from through there.' I point, my hand still shaking.

'Where are the others?' Sam asks looking uneasy.

'Not sure,' says Luke.

'I heard someone cry out. I know I did.' I turn to Dominique and look into her large eyes.

'Well let's go and see what the fuss is about, shall we?' Anya states before marching off in the direction I pointed to. Eventually we all follow suit.

At the far end of the sub it is especially dark and cold.

'I think it came from the engine room.' My voice quivers.

As Anya opens the heavy door we are all hit with a metallic smell of blood.

The blue light from above reflects on the pool of thick blood on the floor, giving it a purple tinge. Kneeling over a body is Fiona. The blood has soaked into her trousers and is all over her hands.

'What have you done?' Luke's words echo around the metal room.

'I-I…' Her tear-stained face is illuminated.

'Is he dead?' Sam asks, putting his hand up over his mouth and nose to try and protect himself from the smell.

'I-I…' Fiona continues to stutter.

'I am not staying here.' Dominique turns and rushes away from the bloody scene.

'Who is it?' I ask from the back, unable to really see the body.

'Patrick,' Fiona wails and throws herself over the butchered corpse.

'This is too much, man.' Luke also turns and leaves in a hurry.

'What happened?' Anya bends down. Her face is extremely pale and her eyes brim with tears.

'I don't know,' Fiona sobs, 'I just found him like this.' Snot runs down her top lip.

'This is nuts.' Sam turns to me. 'We've got to get off this fucking thing. There is a psycho on board. I don't trust any of you.'

'You found him?' Anya asks with scepticism but Fiona is too busy looking down at her blood-covered hands to hear.

Getting up, Anya wipes her eyes and carefully steps around Fiona. She bends down beside Patrick and feels for a pulse. Her eyes tell us he is gone. Then she strokes the hair away from his face, revealing his large, open, glassy eyes and rests her hand on his bloody chest. At which point Sam turns and throws up.

The smell of his vomit mixed with the stench of blood makes me want to pass out and I slip away from them all, unable to face it anymore.

Anya

I've always wanted to work with marine life. Even when I was very young, I knew this was my calling and I studied hard at school in Malmö where I grew up. My father was a science teacher and my mother was a seamstress. We lived in a lovely house by the water and I was a very happy child. I had lots of friends and I did well in school. I got good grades in my exams and made it to the University of Gothenburg where I studied marine biology when I was twenty.

I moved to England when I was twenty-four and went to Plymouth University where I did my master's. That is where I met Patrick. Even now, five years later, I find it strange referring to him as Patrick. When we met I knew him as Dr Skuse. He was my lecturer in Plymouth.

Despite his age and slightly scruffy appearance he was attractive. He had eyes as blue as the ocean and he was tall, which I liked.

Some of the other students used to make fun of his hair behind his back, but I thought it suited him like that. It was a bit long, perhaps, and a bit dishevelled but he wore it well.

When I graduated from Plymouth, Patrick was also coming to the end of his time as a guest lecturer. He had been offered an opportunity, on board a commercial submarine, to explore the Norwegian Sea. I was young, ambitious and he knew me well, so he offered me a job working alongside him. I didn't have to think long before accepting his offer.

We have worked together for over a year now and he is an inspiration. His passion for the ocean never fails to impress me. He is a remarkable man.

Things changed though when Fiona joined us. I had always been the centre of his attention and that altered because of her. She is much more pushy than I am. She is a strong woman who knows her mind. The fact that she is closer to his age, I think, makes a difference.

It was only when she appeared that I realised I was in love with Patrick. Up until that point I hadn't known. Although we were not lovers it felt as though he was mine, but then she arrived and I had to get used to sharing him. It was a struggle being in such close proximity to someone I was infatuated with. On the submarine there was no getting away from her or him.

It had been good working side by side with him up until that point. She ruined everything but what made it worse still was that I actually quite liked her. She could be very funny and she was smart. I liked her and I was angry with myself for that.

Despite myself, we started to build a friendship. It was nice having another woman on board when most of my colleagues were men. We would play chess together some evenings, using the set she had brought with her to help pass the long and boring nights.

Fiona had originally been in the navy but, after retiring, decided to get involved with scientific projects that required her to use the skills she'd learnt while serving. She had never married or had children and I used to wonder why until one evening over a tense game of chess I asked her.

'Oh, Anya, didn't you know? I like men and women. I could never choose one over the other. This way I get the best of both worlds.'

I remember blushing when she said it. I hadn't known she was bisexual and it came as a bit of a surprise. I hoped she didn't fancy me.

'Oh, I see,' I said, unable to meet her eye. I tried to focus my attention on the game in hand.

Then one evening a little while later I made a discovery.

I'd been in the living area writing up my notes on the day's findings. The sub was very quiet since most of the crew had gone to bed. I was concentrating hard on making sure that I got all the information down correctly when I heard a sound coming from the control room of the sub. Putting my pen down I got up and went closer to have a better listen. It was a strange sound and I put my ear to the door to try to decipher it. When I still couldn't work out if it was coming from a person or something mechanical I pushed the door open a fraction so that I could see.

To my horror, I saw Patrick and Fiona having sex. He was so busy thrusting into her that he didn't see me standing there – but she did, and she smiled at me and winked. At that point I turned and ran off. I took myself down to the engine room and cried my eyes out. I felt betrayed by them both.

It sickened me that she was such a whore. They weren't even having sex in a bed, just over a seat. How could they?

I sat on the cold metal floor and banged my fists against the wall, my hurt quickly turning to rage. The look she had given me was unforgivable. I'd not mentioned my feelings for Patrick to her but she knew, the way women always just know these things, she knew. To wink at me really was offensive. I thought we were friends. Why had she been so cruel?

This was not the first time in my life that I had come across a woman who I'd liked, and trusted, but who turned out to be a bitch. It made me sad when I accepted that it wasn't likely to be the last time either.

But I was a good person. I worked hard, I was loyal – I didn't deserve this and more than that, Patrick didn't deserve it. He was a good man who had been led astray by the brain in his trousers. Did he even know she swung both ways? If so, didn't he care?

Patrick had always struck me as a monogamist, so what was going on? Then it dawned on me; perhaps he was in love. It had happened to me, stuck down here in this claustrophobic space, why couldn't the same thing have happened to him? But I was devastated that it was her he had fallen for and not me. For a moment I found myself wishing that it had been me, bent over the seat, making him happy and listening to him groan.

For the first time since I'd set foot on the sub I wished I wasn't there. I wanted to be back with my family in Sweden, surrounded by the familiar comfort of home. I missed my mother and father suddenly, even though I hadn't seen them for some time. It was difficult to keep in touch when you spent months away at sea.

Suddenly I longed to be back in my old bedroom, snuggled up in my bedding, inhaling the familiar smell of the washing powder my mother always used. But it was a waste of time, thinking like that. I was not at home. I was in the engine room of a cold metal submarine, drying my eyes while my heart continued to break.

As I got to my feet, still shaking a bit, I realised that before very long I would have to face them both. There was nowhere to hide and the next morning I would be expected to sit with them both over breakfast and pretend nothing had changed. I could just about manage it with Patrick, because he didn't know I'd seen them, but sharing a pot of coffee with Fiona was an entirely different prospect.

Still feeling utterly miserable I made my way into the bunkroom I shared with Fiona and two others and got into my bed.

Lying in the dark, listening to my own breathing, I waited for the door to open and for Fiona to take herself to bed but that sound didn't come until much later. Knowing she had been with Patrick all that time made me want to cry but I refused to let her hear my sadness. She wouldn't take my dignity from me as well as everything else.

All I had to do was make it through the night without crying like a child. The next day would be awful and I needed all my strength to be able to face them both and keep up the pretence that everything was okay. But in my heart I knew it would never be the same again and for the first time since getting on board I felt utterly alone.

The Pica Explorer

Day three. Hour 07:50.

'Another one.' I stumble into the living area where Susie and Frank are sitting at opposite ends of the long Formica table in total silence. Frank is sucking his fingers, having just devoured a tin of baked beans and some sliced bread. The smell of the beans makes me feel sick.

'Another what?' Frank demands, looking irritated.

'Another dead.'

Susie leans forward and wraps her arms around herself, as if for warmth.

'Who?' she asks frantically.

'Patrick. He's dead. There was so much blood.' I put my head in my hands and rub my throbbing temples.

'Blood?' Frank asks, his eyes twinkling.

'Yes. Everywhere.' I close my eyes.

'What happened?' Susie half whispers.

'I don't know.'

'I'm going to go find out what the hell is going on.' Frank stands up banging his fists on the table, before wiping away a smear of bean sauce that has gathered at the corner of his mouth with the back of his hand. 'You two stay here.'

Susie turns away in disgust as Frank barges past me and out of the room.

'Was there some kind of accident?' Susie beckons for me to come and sit down.

'I don't know. I don't think so.' I slump down into the chair, realising that one of my migraines is threatening to come on.

Susie stretches across the table and reaches for a bottle of vodka that is close to Frank's empty bowl, before unscrewing the cap and taking a large gulp.

'Susie! What are you doing?' I exclaim with shock.

'Much better,' she sighs, replacing the cap. 'I needed that.'

We both burst into laughter. It is the kind of laughter that strikes when you are in church and someone farts. It is uncontrollable and hysterical.

Moments later Sam appears in the doorway looking horrified but we cannot help ourselves or stop.

'What is wrong with you?' he hisses.

And suddenly I am not laughing anymore.

'Seriously, have you both gone fucking mad? Crazy bitches.' Sam's good-looking face is now distorted in a grimace.

'Sorry.' Susie has also managed to stop and her cheeks are flushed red.

'Someone cut that man up. Someone stabbed him until he could no longer move. And that someone is on board. You think that's funny, do you?' The words tumble out of him and fill the silence.

'I don't believe it.' Susie reaches for the vodka again but I grab her hand and stop her, shaking my head.

'You'd better believe it, you stupid woman. There is a killer among us. For all I know it could be you.' Sam's pupils have dilated with fear and he stands there looking twitchy, as if he is waiting for the killer to pounce on him.

It is my turn to reach for the vodka and I drink a huge mouthful before offering the bottle back to Susie apologetically.

Sam approaches and comes to sits at the table with us, waiting for Susie to finish her turn before helping himself.

'Might as well get drunk, right.' Sam clings to the bottle, hoping the contents will erase what is happening to us. 'He was the only one who could have got us out of this situation. Now he's dead. We're all fucked.'

Susie's eyes fill with tears and she begins to chew on the sleeve of her cardigan.

'I don't know which is worse,' Sam continues, 'dying at the hands of a fucking psycho or running out of air.'

'Stop it!' Susie shouts suddenly. 'Stop it right now. We are going to get out of here.'

'If you believe that, then you really are thick,' Sam sneers as Frank comes stomping into the room.

'Stupid little shit,' he mutters to himself, paying no attention to the fraught mood in the room. 'He only had one job to do.' Frank snatches the bottle of vodka away from Sam, who recoils like a chastised puppy.

'What are you talking about?' Susie asks cautiously.

'That fucking waste of space Luke. I asked him to get his camera and film in the room where Patrick is lying but he refused. He refused me! He'll never work in this business again.'

'You what?' Sam stands up to face Frank.

'I wanted some shots of the body.' Frank shrugs.

'You really are sick.' Susie looks up at Frank in horror.

'We could have used it for the film. It's not very often you get a chance to shoot something like that, something so raw. It could have looked beautiful on the big screen.' Frank slurps from the bottle.

'I don't want to be in the same room as you.' I get up, putting distance between my body and his, almost tripping over. 'You are a monster.'

'Don't be so melodramatic, doll,' Frank smirks while rolling his eyes. 'It's only a bit of blood.'

'No, Frank, no.' Susie also stands and shakes her head. 'It's more than that. This isn't a prop. This is a person we are talking about. A man who we have all spent time with is now dead. Murdered. You're so cold. Did you do this? Was it you?'

'I'm just trying to make the best of a bad situation.' Frank sits down and for the first time since we met I see a chink in his armour.

'We are all scared,' I say to the silent room just as Dominique comes bursting in, mascara smudged down her cheeks and her eyes wet with tears.

'I'm getting out of here,' she pants. 'I can't stay here a second longer. This place is going to kill us all. I don't want to die. One of you is a killer. I am not going to be a victim. I am going to survive!'

Sam tries to approach her but she won't let him anywhere near. Her eyes are wild and scared. She looks at each of us with fear and suspicion. 'One of you did this to them but you won't do it to me. I won't let you.' Her voice shakes as she looks around desperately for an escape route.

'There is no getting out of here, you silly girl.' Frank sounds tired.

'Yes there is. I am going to get out and none of you can stop me!' she wails as she runs back into the long corridor, her words echoing around the vessel.

'She's lost it.' Frank rubs his eyes with the palms of his hands. 'She has gone fucking stark raving mad.'

'I'm going after her.' Sam springs into action.

'Typical actress,' Frank continues. 'Fucking mad. Be careful, kid, you might be next.'

'There is nothing typical about this,' Susie says following Sam, leaving Frank and me alone.

Not having the energy to give chase, I join Frank at the table. He has another sip of the vodka then hands me the bottle.

I nod in appreciation before helping myself to some more. The vodka is cold and slips down my throat easily.

'Fancy a fuck before you die?' Frank asks as if he might be offering me a biscuit. The idea of it makes me feel quite ill.

'I think I'll pass.' My lip curls in revulsion.

'Your loss, doll.'

'So be it, I'd rather take my chances with a killer.' I get up and leave him alone, suddenly desperate to be anywhere else but in his company.

As I make my way through the sub I realise I am alone and fear hits me hard. I shouldn't be on my own. It's not safe.

Half running, my footsteps reverberate around the metal shell. This only compounds my migraine, which has not been eased by the vodka that sloshes around in my stomach, like the waves in the sea that keeps us all prisoners.

Then a loud clanking sound makes me come to a halt. The noise sounds like metal hammering on metal with some force. The noise makes me hold my breath for a moment. Is the submarine falling apart? Has something crashed into us? Are we sinking further still?

But then I realise that it is coming from inside and I follow the sound as it grows louder, thudding in time with my headache. Seconds later I hear shouting.

'Stop it, Dom!' I recognise Sam's voice. 'You're going to kill us all!'

Moments later I have arrived at the scene of the commotion and discover Dominique smashing a spanner against the door to the outside.

'She's lost her mind.' Susie turns to me.

'Please, Dominique, this isn't going to help. You can't open it. You'll drown us all,' Sam pleads while she continues bashing the door with a strength that surprises us all.

'You have to stop her,' Susie begs Sam to do something but we all know that if he gets too close to her he risks being injured.

'Dominique'—I try to steady my voice—'you have to stop. Put the spanner down. You're frightened and we all understand but this isn't the answer. Please, put it down and let's all talk about it. We can work it out together.'

And just like that she stops banging.

'You really think we can get out?' Her eyes are wild and terrified. 'Do you? How can I trust a word any of you say?'

I can't answer because I don't want to lie, but I also want her to stop.

'You are scaring us. We have to stick together now.'

From nowhere, Sam launches himself at her, tackling her to the ground and knocking the spanner out of her hand. It all happens in slow motion. Her head smashes onto the bend of one of the pipes. The sound reminds me of an egg cracking. Her body falls limp to the ground and begins to twitch as blood seeps out of her skull.

'Oh Jesus, oh fuck.' Sam pushes himself away from her convulsing body.

'What have you done?' Susie rushes over to Dominique and sits helplessly on the ground next to the twitching woman.

'I just wanted her to stop.' Sam's voice is shaking and his face looks paler than before. 'I didn't mean to hurt her.'

Susie removes her cardigan and places it underneath Dominique's head in an attempt to make her more comfortable, but Dominique does not respond and continues to jerk.

It only takes a moment for Susie's cardigan to turn from salmon pink to deep crimson.

'She's losing a lot of blood,' she says. Sam watches from a few feet away, unable to move or help at all.

'This can't be happening.' I hear myself say as the world around me starts to spin again and my legs give way. 'I can't breathe.' I scrabble about on the floor, sucking in air and trying to stop the inevitable from happening.

Sam crawls over to me and puts his arm around my shoulder, pulling me into a foetal position on the floor, with my head resting in his lap.

'Come on,' he says, 'just take deep breaths.' But his breathing is also laboured.

Lying on the floor I watch as Dominique's body stops twitching until finally it is completely still. All that I can hear is my own brain thudding against the walls of my skull. The pain is excruciating and I think my mind might be about to explode out of my head.

Turning my head, I look up at Sam who is staring at Dominique while tears roll down his cheeks, landing on my forehead like a hammer to my brain.

I watch Susie as she rests her head on Dominique's chest, listening for signs of life. Her eyes close slowly as she returns to a sitting position, shaking her head and letting her chin fall to her chest.

Sam's mouth opens and he lets out a scream but I do not hear it. I am deaf to everything except the sound of my mind fracturing, knowing that now three people have died and we have been stranded down here for less than forty-eight hours.

Sam

Getting into acting was easy for me. I am good-looking so I had a head start. That's half the battle, what you look like. I hadn't wanted to be an actor at first. I'd wanted to go into law. From a young age I wanted to be involved with the justice system and when I was ten my mum took me to the Old Bailey. I was so impressed by the grandeur; I'll never forget it.

Watching the lawyer in his wig address the judge and the jury, I remember thinking how in control he was. They all hung on his every word and I thought, at that moment, *I want to grow up and be like him.* Sure, I thought the outfit was a bit silly but I loved the drama of the courtroom.

My mother was an actress and my father was a musician. As a young child I led quite a bohemian life. Mum had starred in some big productions in the West End and got a part in a Broadway show. She had to leave Dad to look after us when she went over to New York for four months. I really missed her but I was also proud. Both my parents taught me to follow my dreams. I grew up thinking that anything was possible if you just put your mind to it.

Life was good until Mum returned from America. I remember it so well.

I was sixteen years old and had just finished my last exam. Dad, my younger brother, Josh, and I all drove from our house in Fulham to Heathrow Airport to collect her. Dad was holding a huge bunch of her favourite flowers, irises, and we all waited with anticipation for her to come through arrivals. We'd spoken on the phone a lot while she was away but it was different in those days – we didn't have FaceTime, not like you do now.

Finally, when she appeared, she was unrecognisable. She'd been thin before she went, but on her return she was as skinny as a rake and had large dark bags under her eyes. She'd also cut all of her long brown hair off and now wore it very short. When she saw us her eyes filled with tears and she smiled but we could all see that she was sad. I didn't understand what was wrong.

We all hugged and made our way back to the car. Josh wouldn't shut up and kept asking questions about her time in the US. He wanted to know all about New York. Mum was patient and answered all of his stupid questions but her voice was full of sadness. I remember Dad and I shared a look. We both knew something wasn't right even if Josh hadn't noticed.

On the drive home there was a strange atmosphere in the car. Josh continued to ask dumb questions but in between, when it was silent, things felt strange. I'd been so looking forward to having her back, the disappointment was a bitter pill to swallow.

Once home she excused herself and said she needed a long bath, to wash away the plane smell that she said was on her clothes. Josh went up to his bedroom to play on his computer and I followed Dad into the kitchen.

'What is wrong with Mum?' I asked, hoping he would have an explanation.

'She's probably just tired. It's quite a long flight, you know,' Dad said while busying himself with some washing-up that was piled in the sink.

'It's more than that.' I sat down at the kitchen table and flicked a crumb onto the floor. 'She isn't herself.'

'I'm sure she'll feel better after her bath,' said Dad, doing his best to convince himself.

When Mum appeared a while later wearing her old dressing gown, I noticed how it hung off her frame. She looked so small in it and Dad commented that she was looking a bit thin. Mum just shrugged it off.

It went on like that for weeks. She was miserable. I'd often hear her crying in the bathroom and at night she would wander around the house, unable to sleep. For a while Dad buried his head in the sand. I guess he was also probably disappointed not to have the old Mum back. But one night that all changed.

Dad had been to the pub with his friends to watch a football game. He returned home a bit pissed at about eleven. Josh and I were upstairs in our rooms and Mum was downstairs staring blankly at the television. I heard the front door go and went to ask Dad what the result was but before I could, I saw him enter the sitting room and close the door. I sat on the stairs listening to their conversation.

'For fuck's sake, Tammy, what is it? What is wrong with you? I just wanted to give my wife a kiss.'

'I'm sorry,' Mum moaned.

'You can't stand to be in the same room as me and you flinch every time I touch you. What is it? Did you meet someone else while you were in America?'

'No, Christ, Jack, no!'

'Well what is it then? You've not been yourself since you came back. I'm not the only one who's noticed. Sam has picked up on it, too. We are worried about you.'

'I can't.' I heard Mum crying.

'You can, love. Just tell me what is wrong. I want to help you, but I can't if you keep shutting me out.'

There was silence and I craned to hear better, not wanting to miss a thing.

'Come on, Tam, this is me. You can tell me anything.' Dad didn't sound so angry anymore. There was another long silence and I found myself holding my breath.

'I was raped.' In that moment those three words had altered the course of my life.

Dad remained quiet.

'A man came into my dressing room, after the show one night, and raped me.'

'Someone raped you…' Dad sounded bewildered. 'Who was it? Why didn't you call me? Did you know him?'

'No. Not really.'

'I'm calling the police.' I wanted Dad to stop and just tell her that she was safe now.

'No, don't! It was my fault. I invited him to my dressing room. He got his wires crossed. I feel stupid enough, please don't call the police. Frank Holden, the producer, approached me after a show one night and told me he wanted to talk to me about a part in a film he was making. I was flattered, excited, I suppose, and it didn't occur to me that I was doing anything wrong, so I told him to come by my dressing room to discuss it. It was my fault.'

'Frank Holden. That bastard! We have to call the police.'

'No, I told you, it's my fault.'

'It wasn't your fault, love.' I heard the tears in Dad's voice and I knew I'd heard enough. Standing up, I rushed back to my bedroom where I lay face down on my bed and cried until I could not cry any more.

The next day was difficult. I had to act as if I didn't know anything. Mum wouldn't have wanted me to hear and I didn't want to tell her that I knew her secret, so I kept it to myself. Part of me wondered if I should let Josh know what had happened to her but I realised no good would come from telling him. He would have to carry the burden too and I didn't want that.

But a few weeks later it all came out.

I came back from sixth form to what I thought was an empty house. Dad had a gig playing with a band on an album and Josh was at school. I called out for Mum, expecting her to be there, but got no answer so went into the kitchen and made myself a sandwich.

It was autumn and there was a hell of a wind blowing. I remember it like it was yesterday.

When I finished my sandwich I picked up my bag, which was heavy with books, and took it up to my bedroom, passing the bathroom on my way. I could hear the branches thrashing on the kitchen window and noticed the sound of the water running. I guessed Mum was in there having a bath. She spent a lot of time in the bathroom.

After putting my bag in my room I went and knocked on the door, just to say hello. There was no answer. I tried again, wondering if the sound of the water had drowned me out but there was still no answer. I started banging loudly on the door and shouting, worried that she might have fallen asleep.

It was only when water started to seep from underneath the door that I knew something was wrong.

Using all my might I ran at the door with my shoulder and burst through into the bathroom.

Lying there, in a bath full of bloody water, was my mother. Her limp arm hung out from one side of the tub and her glazed eyes were staring up at the ceiling. She had large gashes down both her forearms. I rushed to her and tried to pull her out of the bath. I wanted to save her, but it was too late. Instead, I sat on the wet floor holding her hand and cried my heart out. The water continued running.

Dad came home and found us like that. I will never forget his face. At her funeral I made a promise to God that I would avenge her. I vowed that I would find Frank Holden and make him suffer. I knew the quickest way to get to him would be to get into acting. I'd always been quite good at it; I suppose I got that from Mum.

Dad was a bit surprised when I announced that I wanted to take it up and that I didn't want to be a lawyer anymore, but he was too broken by her death to try and change my mind.

I did lots of private tuition and found myself an agent. It was easy, really. Soon I had jobs starring in ads and before long I managed to secure a few auditions and get parts acting in serials. It wasn't long before I got to hear about Frank's new film and persuaded my agent to try and get me an audition. She said she thought it was highly unlikely but promised to give it a go. I don't know which one of us was more shocked when she received the call saying that Frank wanted me to come in and try out for a part.

The first time I met him I was shaking; not from nerves but from anger. I really had to control myself not to punch him in the face. It wasn't easy but I managed. I used some of the acting techniques I'd learnt to get through the audition without giving the game away. He had a big ego and was easy to charm. Once I got over my feelings of anger, I acted my arse off so that I stood a chance of getting the part. I didn't care about the film or the role but I needed the part so that I would have an opportunity to spend more time with him. My plan required me to play the long game and I did just that.

Upon meeting him I wondered if I really had it in me to see the whole thing through, but as soon as I saw the way he looked at Dominique, my co-star, I knew that I could do it and was in no doubt that this man deserved everything that was coming his way. It had taken me twelve years to get to this point and there was no turning back.

My mother had killed herself because of this man and it was his turn to suffer. I had it all planned out, down to the last detail. I would hit him where it hurt him most, his reputation, but what I hadn't counted on was the submarine sinking.

The Pica Explorer

'She's fucking dead.' I can't remember another time I've heard Susie swear and it sounds strange. She is too pure for that kind of language.

Sam looks down at his shaking hands in horror.

'I didn't mean to. I just wanted her to stop.' His voice is breaking and I can hear his hurt.

Susie hangs her head and I watch as her shoulders move up and down while she cries. 'What is happening to us? I can't be near any of you,' she sobs.

I manage to sit up and take some deep breaths, backing away from Dominique's body as the pool of blood from her head starts to move closer to me.

'Three.' My voice is hoarse. 'Three people are dead.'

'We have to go and tell the others.' Susie looks up, her eyes brimming with tears.

'No. No, we can't.' Sam's words are full of panic. 'They'll think it's me. They'll think I did it.'

'You did do it! You're a killer,' Susie shrieks, pointing at the lifeless body lying on the metal floor.

'No, it was an accident. I haven't killed anyone. Not on purpose. They'll think I did the others.' Sitting quite still I watch Sam closely. Was it really an accident? He doesn't strike me as a cold-blooded killer but, then again, none of the people on board fit that description.

I try to think straight for just one minute but my mind is a fog and I can't settle on a single train of thought. My brain continues to thud.

'I'm not staying here.' Susie gets to her feet. 'We need to tell the others.'

Sam grabs her long skirt and prevents her from moving.

'I'm begging you.' His knuckles are white and his fists cling to the fabric.

'I don't have a choice.' Susie puts her small pale hands over his and encourages him to release her. 'I will tell them it was a mistake.' She puts her hand on his head and ruffles his hair before leaving us in the corridor, her brown leather boots echoing around us as she walks away.

'Help me hide her.' Sam turns to me, his eyes filled with desperation.

'No, Sam. You have to face it. We can't hide her. She's not a mistake you can just sweep under the carpet.' I feel for him as I watch his face crumble. If he is the killer, he is doing a good job of faking remorse.

'It wasn't meant to be like this. She wasn't meant to die. Why did she have to be so stupid? If she'd opened the hatch it would have killed us all. What was she thinking? I was just trying to protect everyone.' He stands up and slams his hands against the cold wall in anger. 'How can it all have gone so wrong?'

'She wasn't thinking straight. She was scared and panicking. She would never have been able to open the hatch anyway. The pressure from the water would have made it impossible.' I look over at the dead girl, feeling real pity for her, as Sam makes a fist and hits the metal shell of the submarine.

'Stop it.' I put my hands up over my ears and close my eyes tightly shut. The noise he is making is piercing my brain like a bullet. 'Stop it!' I shout again.

When I can no longer feel the vibrations running through my body, I open my eyes to find myself alone with the body. Sam has disappeared. Perhaps he's gone after Susie.

On my hands and knees I crawl over to Dominique. Her large eyes are open and staring. I gently raise my hand towards her face and close her eyelids. She has seen enough already.

Then, when I have enough strength to stand, I rearrange her body so that she is lying straight, with her legs closed and her arms by her sides. It is the only thing I can do for her now. She looks so young all of a sudden.

'Goodnight, pretty girl.' I wipe the hair from her forehead before reaching for the spanner and tucking it into the back of my trousers. Whether or not Sam intended to hurt her, I don't know; but the fact remains that there is a killer on board and any one of us could be next.

I feel spooked being alone with her body and decide to go find the others. I don't know where Sam has gone and I don't want to chase after him. *Power in numbers*, I think to myself as I make my way through the semi-darkness making sure I keep one hand firmly on the spanner by my back.

The whole body of the sub seems to groan and I drop to the floor, terrified of it caving in above my head. The sound goes on for a few seconds before dissolving again and my world returns to a half reality.

Standing up again I crouch slightly as I make my way along the maze of corridors, still frightened by the noise I heard.

The bodies are now not the most important thing on my mind – our dire situation comes right to the forefront and I start to feel as if I am drowning in my own thoughts.

'Somehow, we need to get the submarine to the surface. Somehow, we have to survive.' I repeat the words to myself over and over again like a mantra, willing it to happen. 'If I believe it, it will be so.'

My throat feels painfully dry and I stop talking to myself, determined to try and save my energy for a more worthwhile purpose.

When I enter the living area I find the others with Susie, who is completely hysterical.

Luke, who is trying to help calm her down, is holding her in a bear-like grip, trying to stop her from hurting herself. She wails and thrashes about in his arms like a rag doll for some time before she no longer has the strength to fight and flops into submission. He has a vacant look on his face.

'Where is Sam? Is it true you saw him kill Dominique?' Luke asks, laying a weak Susie down on one of the benches by the dining table.

'I don't know. He ran off.' It feels as if there are splinters of glass stuck in my gullet.

'Right, from now on we all stay together. No one goes off alone. I'm the fucking director on board this shit-show and I pay your wages,' Frank barks trying to convince himself, and all of us, that he is still in charge.

'Pay our wages?' Luke chuckles. 'That's funny.'

'Why?' Frank's eyes are burning with rage.

'Because none of us are getting out of here alive so your money doesn't mean shit.' The room falls silent. I bet no one has ever spoken to Frank like that before.

'Carry on like that, sunshine, and you definitely won't be getting out of here.' Frank steps up to Luke and shoves his face up close to Luke's.

'Sit the fuck down, old man.' Luke pushes Frank, who is taken by surprise and loses his balance, falling backwards into a chair.

'Stop it,' Susie moans.

'She's right,' Fiona agrees. 'This isn't helping. We will get out of here. There is every chance we will be rescued.'

'You keep telling yourself that,' Luke sneers.

'What do you suggest? Please tell us.' Frank folds his arms across his chest and glares at Luke, who is flushed with rage. Then he turns to Fiona.

We are all looking at her, waiting for an answer, and Fiona looks at each of us in turn.

'I think Frank is right. We must all stay in the same room. We'll be much safer if we do.'

'What if I need the toilet?' Anya asks.

'Then we go together in pairs.'

'Be just my luck I end up going for a shit with a murderer for company. I don't want to die on the crapper.' Luke is still boiling with anger.

'That isn't funny.' I sit down next to Susie and start to stroke her back in a soothing motion.

'None of this is funny,' Fiona says, putting her face in her hands and letting out a loud sigh.

'You look tired,' Anya adds.

'I am tired. We are all tired,' Fiona snaps back.

'Let's try and eat something. We need to think clearly and we need energy to do so.'

'I must admit I'm hungry,' Luke says, beginning to calm down.

'Fine. Go and get some food then. You two.' Frank points at Anya and Luke, still trying to direct.

'I'm not eating anything any of you give me.' Luke looks around us.

Anya sighs and then sets off towards the food storage room. No one mentions the body that is lying in the freezer in that room.

'Where is that little scrote Sam?' Frank demands.

'He ran off,' I say. 'He's frightened.

'Or guilty,' Susie mumbles.

'What are we going to do about Dominique?' Someone has to bring it up.

'Freezer?' Frank suggests coldly.

'Is there room?' I ask.

'Yes. There will be,' Fiona answers gravely.

'Wait for her to get back with supplies then you can sort it out,' Frank says, picking his teeth with a fat finger and pointing at us all.

'I am not your employee.' Fiona stands up proudly, straightening her top. 'I don't take orders from you.'

'That's fine, doll, but you'd better not complain when the kid starts stinking the place out.'

Child

When Mummy met Nick everything settled down for a while. He seemed to make her happy. I'd never seen her happy, or with a man, so it took some time for me to accept that it had happened.

The beatings stopped because her attention was focused elsewhere. I know it sounds strange but I actually felt even less loved than before. When Nick entered her life she stopped noticing me. She didn't have time to get cross. It was like I didn't exist at all and although I was pleased that she stopped hurting me, I missed her attention.

Nick was a short man, with broad shoulders and a bald head. He reminded me a bit of a garden gnome. Mummy was as tall as him. She told me he was a builder.

They would go out in the evenings and leave me alone in the house. I'd get my own dinner, usually some beans and toast or a jam sandwich, if the jar wasn't empty, then sit on the floor in the living room and watch TV for a while before going up to bed for eight o'clock.

When they came home I'd hear them coming up the stairs and hide under my duvet, holding my breath and hoping they wouldn't come in and find me awake but they never checked. I could have been dead and no one would have known.

Mummy always used to come into my room to make sure I was asleep. So much had changed.

Lying in my bed, listening to the sound of my own breathing, I started to hear another noise, coming from somewhere else in the house. A grunting, panting, moaning that was getting louder and louder. I was frightened and didn't know what was happening.

Rolling the covers down I peered into the darkness hoping to make sense of the sound. Then, moments later there was a banging on the *far wall of my room. It was coming from the other side. It was coming from Mummy's bedroom.*

Getting out of bed, my naked feet found the cold floorboards and I crept carefully towards the wall and put my ear against it.

The moaning was getting louder and I could hear both Mummy and Nick making strange noises. At first I thought they were fighting but it didn't sound like she was in pain. Then finally Nick let out a long, low, groan and the banging stopped. I waited, for a moment, frozen to the spot, wondering what was happening. Then I heard laughter and rushed back to my bed, frightened and confused. I didn't understand how two people who sounded like they were in pain could then begin laughing.

Listening to Mummy laugh felt odd. She rarely laughed before Nick came into our lives. It made me feel guilty that I could never make her happy.

That would not be the last time I would hear them. It would not be the last time I went back to bed and fell asleep with my hands over my ears.

Frank

I'd always wanted to get into the movie business. I did okay at school but learning never really interested me. I liked action. As a kid I'd been keen on photography. When I was sixteen my parents gave me a camera and I guess you could say that is where it all started.

Being a Jewish kid in England in the seventies wasn't easy. I had to quickly learn how to look after myself. Despite the fact my parents weren't Hassidic I still had it tough. My father wore a skullcap so everyone knew.

My grandparents had come over to England when my papa was just young. They'd fled Slovakia to escape the Nazis. My grandfather had arrived with little but the clothes on his back. But he was a smart man and had made friends with other Jews who were involved in the antiques trade. Like my grandfather before him, he became an antique dealer and Mum worked in a bakery. We lived in a cottage and I went to the local school. I was an only child and Mum doted on me.

When my father died suddenly of a heart attack, aged forty-two, all that changed. She became very sad and lost all pride in her appearance. Thankfully, Papa left a healthy amount of money in his will so we never went without, but at a tender age of seventeen I became the man of the house.

I'd left school at sixteen in order to follow my dream of becoming a professional photographer and started to get gigs taking pictures behind the scenes of commercials. I was plucky and ambitious and soon enough a director took me under his wing. He started to teach me all about the industry and let me get to grips with the film cameras and lighting. He saw something in me, I suppose, and I liked him.

After a few years of working as a runner behind the scenes I decided I wanted more. Being a director's skivvy wasn't enough. I didn't like taking orders and knew I could do a better job than some of the monkeys I was working under.

Realising I wasn't reaching my full potential, I started to put myself forward for other jobs. It was easier in those days than it is now. As long as you had the right friends in the right places you could climb the ranks; provided you had talent, and I had plenty of that.

Ma, who had grown very grey, soon stopped working at the bakery but I was making enough money to ensure she was well looked after. Papa's inheritance had dwindled when I decided to go it alone and start my own film distribution company. It took a while to get off the ground but eventually people started to take notice and I began to build a name for myself.

By the eighties my firm was really taking off. I was in my late twenties and professionals in the industry started to recognise my hard work — and me.

I was given my first opportunity to be an assistant producer for an independent British film in 1983. The film was a hit and catapulted me into the limelight.

It was during that time I met Bob Watkins, the infamous Hollywood producer. He told me he was looking for a young fresh-faced producer to join his company, Watfilms. I jumped at the chance and soon left the UK, headed for LA and stardom. It broke my mother's heart, but I'd given her so many years and now it was time for me to focus on myself. I promised her she would never want for anything and arranged for money to be sent to her every month.

Six months after I left England she died. I didn't attend her funeral. I was busy shooting and couldn't take the time off. She wouldn't have minded anyway, she was dead.

In LA I found the acceptance I'd craved but had never received in London. It didn't matter that I was Jewish, or young, in America, and I quickly embraced their way of life.

The champagne, cocaine and sex flowed over there like water and I enjoyed each with relish.

You will never know how many beautiful women I got to meet on a daily basis. It was like an alien world where only the gorgeous existed and the ugly did not. I was like a pig in muck. Models, actresses, pop stars all threw themselves at me, hoping for parts in my next film and any woman who scorned my advances soon found themselves unable to find work. It was that easy – like shooting fish in a barrel.

By eighty-nine Watfilms was the most powerful independent studio in the States. We were gods of the industry, only taking on the biggest films and working with the very best.

I dined in the top restaurants, shopped in designer stores and lived a life of luxury. I'd made it.

In between producing blockbusters I indulged my love of art-house films and cut my teeth as a director. They were the best days of my life.

In ninety-one I married Lauren Newham, a pretty young thing from Idaho who had the best pair of tits I'd ever seen and who acted in a steamy thriller I produced. We had fun for a while but she didn't appreciate my extracurricular activates and the marriage ended in divorce eighteen months later. I swore after that I'd never marry again. Neither cohabiting nor monogamy suited me. My love lies with making films and I didn't have room for a woman in my life full time. They were handy accessories that came in useful now and again. The rest of the time they were a fucking nuisance.

After years spent in Hollywood I was given the opportunity to direct a big budget television series, set in the UK, so I returned to England and accepted the work.

The drama series, based on a book, centred on a world where witches, kings, queens and dragons resided. It focused on the wars between the various factions and was fantasy fiction at its very best.

Although some of the larger production houses passed up on it, I knew it would do well. It was a violent look into another world. It had everything – sex, war and triumph over evil. It was destined to be a winner and, in reality, I fancied a change from motion pictures. A series would give me a new challenge and another opportunity to show that I could turn my hand to anything I fancied.

After many meetings and long months of persuasion, I persuaded Warner Brothers to get behind the project and invest heavily. Some thought it was a gamble but I knew better. Frank Holden didn't do flops.

The only term that Warners insisted on was having a young up-and-coming director on board. I was to be the producer and that was fine with me. Finally, after months of planning, we began filming in the Highlands. The weather was miserable but the setting was perfect for the opening scene.

I bought an apartment in central London and used it as my base; although, during shooting I spent many nights in hotels around the country.

During the filming of the first episode we had only one problem – the writer. Jackson Miles, who'd written the book, became very insistent that he should be involved in the making of the programme. Not wanting to upset the author, Warners agreed to allow him to become involved in the scriptwriting. It was a huge mistake. The geeky little author, who most likely grew up playing *World of Warcraft* and masturbating furiously, didn't have a clue about screenwriting and managed to upset every writer who worked on the show.

In the end I took the little worm aside and gave him a piece of advice. 'Look, Jackson,' I said putting my arm round his weedy shoulder, 'leave this to the big boys. Fuck off back to your pit and write more books.'

I don't think anyone had ever spoken to him like that. That is the big problem with this industry, everyone is so set on playing it nice and sucking up. I saw things differently. He was interfering with my work and my show and I wasn't going to stand for it.

The next day Jackson emailed Warners and said that he no longer wished to be involved. Everyone breathed a huge sigh of relief and work started again without any further interruptions.

In ten weeks we'd managed to shoot the entire first series and when it aired, three months later, the fans went nuts for it and rave reviews poured in. I was hailed a genius, naturally, but it was unfortunate having to share my crown with the director, a kid out of film school who didn't know his arse from his elbow. That irritated me and I decided that he was a fly which needed swatting. I made it my business to do just that.

During the filming of the second series I made sure that I spent as much time with Ralph, the director, as possible. I befriended the little creep and started inviting him to join me for drinks in the evenings. The fresh-faced little fucker, who bordered on being arrogant, was in awe that a man of my standing wanted to take him under my wing. It was so easy – like taking candy from a repulsive little baby.

One evening, after a few expensive measures of brandy from my own collection, I offered him some cocaine. It was a gamble. I didn't know if he was one of those clean-living little shits from Shoreditch or whether he would indulge, but I thought it worth the risk.

As soon as I'd cut the lines on the coffee table the pig had his nose right in there hoovering it all up. I produced more and more of the stuff, making sure I did very little, and watched as he filled up on the drug.

A lot of people do cocaine. It's no big deal, especially in Hollywood, but most people don't get hold of good stuff. The powder they buy is cut to shit and mixed with rat poison, or speed if they are lucky. But I was rich and had contacts that could get hold of the purest stuff, and the good stuff, let me tell you, is in a different league to the pub grub that most of the great unwashed shove up their nostrils.

Ralph was high after a few lines but I kept racking it up until he was on another planet.

Then at six in the morning, when he looked like a ghost with huge dilated pupils, I kicked him out of my hotel room and reminded him we needed to be on set in fifteen minutes. The look on his face was priceless.

Needless to say, during filming that day he was a mess and everyone on set could see it.

That evening I dropped Warners an email telling them that I was concerned Ralph had a drug habit. It was as easy as that. It only took one evening for me to put his career in jeopardy.

The next day filming was put on hold and Ralph was called into a meeting with Warners. If I could have rubbed my hands together like a panto villain I would have done.

Expecting to hear that Ralph had been sacked from the show, I was disappointed when I heard nothing. Still, filming was on hold and before long the crew and cast began to get worried about the lack of communication from the studio. I myself began to think that the silence from HQ wasn't looking good.

Two days later I received an email from the head of Warners asking me to attend a meeting in London. This was it. I knew they'd sacked Ralph and were going to ask me to step in as director.

I went into the meeting full of beans but left it distraught. It seemed the little arsehole had told them I had been the one to ply him with the drugs and Warners, not wanting to act on hearsay, had done some digging and discovered from other 'unnamed sources' that I did indeed often take the drug. During the meeting they told me that I was no longer going to be producer on the show and that if I went quietly they would keep my indiscretion away from the tabloids. What choice did I have? I left the show and returned to my London apartment under a cloud.

***

Despite assurances from Warners that my indiscretion wouldn't be made public, the work started to dry up and I felt I was being shunned by the industry. I still had friends, of course, but I knew that something had changed. You know when you're being cut out.

I'd been used to calling up buddies and planning to make a movie and suddenly that had changed. All thanks to that little maggot Ralph. What sort of name was Ralph for a pathetic scrawny white kid from Bristol?

After a few months of feeling sorry for myself because things were quiet, I decided to pull myself out of the slump.

Something I've always done to pass the time is read; and during those months I read a lot. One of the books was a graphic novel called *Below the Surface*. A small indie press had seen the potential in the writer and the merit in the story and had published it. I'd come across it by chance, flicking through recommendations on Amazon. The first thing that grabbed me was the cover – a very graphic image of blood and water mixing together on a plain white background. I loved the blue and red. It reminded me of a horror film called *Event Horizon*, in which the director had colour graded the film so that the reds and blues in each scene stood out. It worked beautifully and made for a very visual viewing experience. Not exactly Oscar-winning stuff but memorable nonetheless, and a classic, in my opinion, from the point of view of the use of colour on screen. Presumably it was that cerebral link that drew me to *Below the Surface*.

It wasn't Shakespeare by any stretch of the imagination but, much like the cover, it painted pictures in my mind while I was reading. There was no doubt that this book needed to be turned into a film and there was no doubt that I was going to be the man to do it. Sure, it was going to be a challenge, not just because my popularity was at an all-time low, but also because much of the action took place on a submarine.

Finding the funding, crew and actors would be easy. Where I knew I'd struggle would be getting my hands on a sub. Then I remembered I'd worked with a man who'd been involved in marine wildlife documentaries a few years back. There was no guarantee that he'd be able to help but it was a starting point at least, and I set about finding the contact information for a man whose name escaped me. I'd always relished a challenge and this was going to be just that. Besides, it was the perfect distraction from thinking about how to get my own back on that little turd Ralph. Suddenly revenge was the last thing on my mind and I felt better than I had done in months. Now, at last, I had bigger fish to fry again.

The Pica Explorer

Day three. Hour 09:00.

When Sam reappears we all gaze at him with distrust.
'Where have you been?' Susie inquires.
'It was an accident.' Sam's face is gaunt.
'So you say,' Frank snorts.
'Okay, this is what we are going to do.' Fiona stands up, calmly tucking her hair behind her ears. 'We need to try to get the sub up to the surface.'
'I hadn't thought of that,' Frank puts in.
'We need power. We have approximately four days of air left at best.'
The room falls quiet and Frank's mouth forms a straight, tight-lipped line.
'The emergency lights won't last four days, and soon the lights will go out. We need to act now before we are plunged into total darkness.'
I nod, feeling like there might be an ounce of hope for the first time since this nightmare began.
'So what do we do?' Luke steps forward.
'We need to use the working batteries on board to get the motor and control systems working again. Let's split into groups.'
'I'm not sure that's a good idea. We still don't know what's going on.' Susie's face is pale and wary.
'It will save time.' Fiona dismisses her concerns, doing her utmost to remain stoic. 'I can work on the wiring and maybe, just maybe, we stand a chance of getting out of here.'

Frank claps his hands. 'That's decided then. But I have to say, doll, it's a shame you didn't say this earlier.'

'It's taken me this long to work out why we sank. These vessels are complicated bits of machinery. It appears there was a leak, which caused a short circuit that meant we lost power.'

'Do you know where the leak is?' Anya asks, fixing Fiona with a cold stare.

'I've got a good idea. Anya, you know this sub well. You take the first group and go and collect as many batteries as you can. Take them from any equipment that isn't vital and bring them back here. I will go to the second level and do the same. Frank, you come with Luke, Zara and me. Susie, Sam, you go with Anya. We meet back here'—she checks her wristwatch—'in forty-five minutes.'

'Maybe the fucker killing everyone did something to the sub,' Frank interrupts, his eyes burning into Sam's face.

'You're not serious?' Fiona spins to face him.

'Why not? Surely it's crossed your mind too.' Frank glares at us all.

'Okay.' I refuse to entertain him and look over at Luke, feeling unhappy that he is part of the group I have been assigned to. I hardly know Fiona, who I have found to be a cold fish, and as for Frank, well, enough said. I wish I could go with Susie.

'Follow me.' Fiona, who has assumed the position of captain, leaves the living area and the three of us trail after her.

I was never good at physics at school and hope that neither she nor the others expect me to be able to contribute to this mission. Still, I'm glad not to be left alone when there is still a killer on board.

As we make our way through the maze of passages I wonder if one of my three companions could be responsible for the murders. Trying to make sense of the bizarre three days we've spent trapped on the ocean floor, I can't help but be suspicious of Frank. He's the only one with a real temper. He's the only one who is angry and strong enough to kill another man in cold blood. But the question that swirls around my head is why. Why would Frank want to kill Ray or Patrick? Is it a coincidence that two men have been murdered? Then I think about what happened to Dominique. I was there. I saw Sam try to stop her endangering all of our lives. It was an accident. Wasn't it?

Above us the lights flicker.

'We don't have much time,' Fiona calls, picking up the pace.

'You really think you can pull this off?' Frank sounds sceptical.

'It's worth a try.'

As we come to another entrance my foot catches on a metal step and I tumble forward, landing flat on my face and catching my head on a sharp corner as I fall.

'Are you okay?' Luke, who was only a few steps ahead, comes to my aid. 'You're bleeding.' He puts his hand up to my temple and presses against the gaping wound. 'Fiona, stop!' he calls out and his words echo around the metal all around us. 'Zara's hit her head.'

'I'm fine.' Sitting on the cold hard floor I push his hand away, and see the shimmer of my blood on his hand, reflecting purple in the blue light.

'You need a bandage on that.' Fiona appears, standing over me. 'There is a first aid kit in the periscope room. I'll be back in a moment.'

'Stupid,' Frank mutters to himself shaking his head.

'I beg your pardon?' Fiona whips around to look at him.

'Stupid girl.' Frank points down at me.

'It was a mistake.' Luke jumps to my defence and I'm grateful to him for doing so. I feel foolish enough as it is without Frank pointing it out.

'It's dark down here. I didn't know there was a step.' I am holding my sleeve against the side of my head, feeling the warm blood seeping into my jumper. The lights flicker again.

'We don't have time for this. We need to get back up to the surface,' Frank barks, grabbing hold of Fiona by the wrist.

'Let go of me now.' Fiona is not intimidated by Frank, but I think she should be.

'It's okay. You two go ahead. I'll make my way to the periscope room and find the first aid kit. Frank is right.' It pains me to have to admit it.

'I'll stay with her.' Luke puts his hand on my shoulder as Frank lets go of Fiona and straightens his posture, while I wonder how safe I will be with Luke.

'Fine.' Fiona doesn't look thrilled at the prospect of being alone with Frank but doesn't have much choice. 'The kit is in a green plastic box on the wall near the ladder. There should be disinfectant and bandages in there. Go back to the living quarters when you've got cleaned up.'

* * *

Half an hour later we are back in the living area and my head is throbbing. The side of my face is beginning to swell and my left eye is closing.

'What happened?' Susie rushes over as they return from their search.

'I tripped and fell.' My cheeks flush red.

'It looks nasty,' Anya comments with no emotion. She is so clinical in her delivery.

'I think you should go for a lie down.' Susie rubs my back delicately with her bony hand.

'No. I want to stay here,' I disagree, despite feeling a wave of fatigue and light-headedness flood over me.

'Any luck?' Luke asks, holding a steaming cup of tea in his hands.

'Yes. We found batteries.' Anya plonks a bag down on the table with a thud. 'Where are the others?'

'We got separated,' Luke explains. 'I had to take Zara to find a first aid kit. Fiona and Frank went looking for more batteries.'

'They are late,' Anya remarks, checking her wristwatch. 'She said forty-five minutes.' This appears to annoy Anya rather than concern her.

'I hope everything is alright.' Susie looks worried. 'Maybe they are in trouble.'

'Should we go and look for them?' Sam suggests.

'You can,' Anya snorts, folding her arms across her chest. 'Fiona can take care of herself.'

'I wouldn't fancy her chances if she came up against Frank.' Sam shrugs, sits down and starts picking the skin around his fingernails.

Closing my eyes I lean back and rest my head on the wall. My eye feels so swollen and tender.

'You don't look well.' Susie puts her cold hand on my forehead. 'Please go and lie down. Just for a little while.'

Feeling weak, I am unable to resist her suggestion.

'Okay. Maybe just for ten minutes.'

Susie and Luke help me to my feet and, standing either side of me, they accompany me towards the sleeping quarters. My legs feel heavy and I start to worry I am going to faint. The smell of blood from my wound seems suddenly very pungent and fills my nostrils.

'I think I am going to be sick.' I stop and bend over as my mouth fills with saliva.

'Deep breaths,' Susie soothes, scraping my hair away from my face while the corridor around me begins to spin.

I can feel Luke standing there watching me. It makes me feel uncomfortable. I hate appearing so weak and vulnerable but I am powerless to do anything to help myself. It's more than that. I know one of these people is a killer.

'I'm sorry,' I moan as my stomach clenches into a ball and the vomit starts to work its way up my throat before pouring out of me and splashing onto the corridor floor. As I wipe the remains of the sick from my mouth, using the sleeve that is coated in dry blood, I hear Luke gag.

'Let's get her to a bed.' Susie hooks her arm underneath mine and Luke does the same on the other side, taking care not to stand in the puddle of bile that lies stinking on the floor.

'I'm not even drunk.' I manage a small smile and allow them to support me as we make our way towards the sleeping quarters.

Once there they lower me onto a bunk. The beds aren't comfortable but I feel instantly at ease as my head makes contact with the pillow.

'Thank you,' I mutter, sounding like someone else. Even as I allow the darkness to take hold and consume me in a deep, feverish slumber, I am praying that I am not murdered in my sleep.

Child

*I*t went on like that for weeks. *Mummy and Nick were happy
and spent lots of time in her bedroom at night, grunting together
and laughing. I kind of got used to the sound but I didn't like
it – not one little bit.*

*One night, after the sounds from Mummy's bedroom next door
had stopped, I heard footsteps on the landing and saw a shadow
lurking outside of my bedroom door. I pulled the duvet up over my
nose and waited, holding my breath. The door handle began to turn
slowly and light flooded into my room making me wince. There, in
the doorway, stood Nick in silhouette. He looked so much bigger than
usual and I wondered why he'd come to my room. He'd never set foot
inside it before.*

*'Hello there.' He stepped inside and closed the door behind him,
plunging us into darkness. 'I thought I'd come and tell you a bedtime
story.'*

*Nick came over to my bed and sat on the end, wearing nothing
but his underwear.*

'Do you like stories?'

I couldn't speak. My throat felt dry.

*'I like stories.' He put his hand on the covers over my leg and gave
my thigh a squeeze. I didn't like it. His hands were strong and his
grip was firm.*

'Where's Mummy?' I managed to whisper.

*'Sleeping. Just like a princess.' He ran his tongue over his lips and
released my leg. 'So, would you like to hear a story?'*

*Something didn't feel right. He shouldn't be in my room this late at
night. I wanted to call out for Mummy but couldn't find the courage.*

'So, once upon a time,' he began, 'there was a child who lived in a house. At night the house was cold and dark. One night, while the mother slept, a big friendly giant came into the house to see the child. The big friendly giant was lonely and wanted someone to talk to. Now the child, who had not seen a giant before, was scared. But the giant was gentle and explained to the child that it just wanted to be friends.

'Every night for a week the giant would creep into the house and talk to the child. The child, who was also lonely, soon realised that the giant meant no harm and began to trust the giant.' Nick paused and sucked in a deep breath.

'What happened next?' I asked, sitting up in bed.

'Well, the giant told the child all about a special hug that would make the giant really happy. The child had never been hugged before and wanted to make the giant happy, so the giant taught the child all about the special hug.'

I could see the sweat glistening on Nick's bald head and wondered why he was sweating when I felt so cold.

'The giant explained how the special hug was something that only giants and children were allowed to do, and he told the child that the hug had to be a secret or the giant wouldn't be able to come and visit the child again, and the child would get into trouble. Now, the thought of never seeing the giant again made the child sad so the child agreed to keep the special hugs a secret.'

'What was the special hug?' I was desperate to know.

'Would you like me to show you?' I watched Nick's hairy chest rising and falling.

'Does it hurt?' I asked, feeling afraid again.

'No.' Nick smiled through nicotine-stained teeth. 'Hugs don't hurt,' he said as he peeled back the duvet leaving me exposed in just my pants.

'It's cold.' I could feel the fine hairs on my arms standing up.

'My hug will make you feel all warm.' Nick placed his hands on my pale shoulders and pulled me into him. 'There, that's nice, isn't it?' His arms were tight around me and I found it hard to pull away.

'Don't struggle.' Nick grabbed the back of my head, holding my hair tightly in his fist, and buried his face into my neck. 'The special hug hasn't finished yet.'

Fiona

After a few years spent cutting my teeth in the navy I decided I wanted out. Working so closely with so many men had been thrilling at first but I soon grew tired of the politics that revolved around being a woman. Not that I was the only female on board, but I was attractive and headstrong, which worked sometimes to my advantage but often against me.

The senior officers were the worst. One in particular really had it in for me. She was an unattractive dumpy thing, with piggy eyes, dry frizzy blonde hair and a nose that would scare the crows.

I put up with it for as long as I could but grew tired of constantly feeling her watchful eye wherever I went. Heaven knows why she had it in for me. Maybe she was jealous. Hell, maybe she fancied me.

When I decided I'd had enough of the navy I felt like a weight had shifted. The navy had let me see the world and given me confidence to believe in myself, but I felt as if I'd outgrown life on board surrounded by so much testosterone.

I returned to Britain after months spent at sea and decided to look for work in another field. My experience meant that I was suited to life at sea and for a while I worked on a private yacht, sailing a millionaire around the southern French coast. The work was easy, the money was good and the weather was better, but I grew bored and craved more adventure.

A few months later I heard through a friend that a position had become available on board a scientific explorer submarine and quickly put myself forward. I learnt, that if I were offered the job, I would be working closely with a small team who were mapping the ocean bed around Greenland and researching the marine life in those waters.

Having spent enough time with the super-rich, being on board with down-to-earth scientists sounded like a dream, so I made my way to Liverpool for the interview.

I'd spoken to Patrick on the phone and he sounded like a nice man, so I wasn't daunted when I met him for the first time. He was good-looking and very different to the suave millionaire and the navy officers I'd been used to dealing with. Patrick was a breath of fresh air. He was laid back and comfortable with himself without being arrogant. I took an instant liking to him.

In this business you don't apply for a job in the same way you have to in other industries. As soon as I'd spoken to Patrick and he'd seen my CV it was all pretty straightforward. The position was mine if I wanted it and we just had to meet to work out the finer details.

I listened intently as Patrick talked me through his career to date, and was fascinated by the life he'd led. His passion for the sea was tangible and inspiring. It is safe to say that I was looking forward to working with him from the start.

My first few weeks on board The Pica Explorer were not as smooth sailing as I'd hoped, thanks to Anya, a fellow scientist, who had worked with Patrick for some time and clearly had a soft spot for him. She saw me as a threat and was extremely frosty from the moment I stepped on board. Having left behind one angry bitch in the navy, I wasn't over the moon to find I'd landed a job working with another.

I understood she felt threatened, especially since Patrick and I quickly built up a rapport, but it was clear to me that her feelings for him were not reciprocated so I really couldn't understand why she was so cold to me. At that stage, Patrick and I only participated in some gentle flirting and I learnt quickly not to do so around Anya, who would glare at me with her snake-like eyes. It gave me the willies.

After a while I got tired of getting the cold shoulder from her. I'd done nothing wrong. In fact, I was second-in-command and I grew irritated by her snide remarks and icy stares. Her behaviour towards me only encouraged me to do everything in my power to wind her up. I'd had enough of jealous women to last me a lifetime and Anya Olsson was not going to get the better of me.

Having reached the end of my tether, I proceeded to flirt shamelessly with Patrick who, I was glad to discover, enjoyed the attention and flirted back.

As for the other people we were working with, none of them seemed to mind in the slightest, which I could see wound Anya up even more.

Then one evening, while I was sitting playing chess with Patrick, it dawned on me that I was actually falling in love with the man. No longer was my flirting an attempt to piss off Anya. I realised I had strong feelings for him and it hit me like a fist to the stomach. I'd had relationships before but this felt different – larger, somehow.

So, when I had the opportunity to kiss him, I made my move. Despite the age gap it felt natural and right. I knew then that I would love him for the rest of my life. The fact that our budding romance would annoy Anya was merely a bonus.

At the start of the affair we took things slowly. Being trapped on board a submarine with other people wasn't the most romantic place to start a relationship and privacy was hard to come by. We'd steal moments together, kissing in the engine room or having a fumble in the bathroom but it wasn't easy to keep it hidden from the rest of the crew.

Naturally, I wanted to shout it from the rooftops. I was in love and it felt great. In some ways, the secrecy added to the excitement of it all. We were like love-struck teenagers sneaking around trying to steal moments together in dark corners, and for some time we managed to keep it to ourselves.

Then, one evening, Anya discovered us having sex.

Her face when she walked in. Well, it was awful. I'd never meant to hurt her so badly. I'd just been sick of her attitude. When she saw us together she was horrified. Of course, I'd been deeply embarrassed by the whole thing and later on had tried to talk to her but she refused to listen. She called me a slut and said that she knew I was using Patrick to make her jealous. I wasn't about to admit that she had been right, because now things had changed, but I couldn't explain that to her. She marched off leaving me feeling dirty and cheap.

Thankfully, Patrick had not been aware of her presence when we'd been having sex and I decided it was best if he didn't know. What good would it have done? He would have felt awkward and it was clear to me he had no idea of her feelings for him. They still had to work together so I decided to keep my mouth shut and absorb all her negative attention myself. I'd made my bed and it was time I lay down in it.

Having said that, despite the tension with Anya, my relationship with Patrick was going strong and I'd never been happier. I was just sorry that she couldn't be happy for us.

The Pica Explorer

Day three. Hour 16:15.

When I wake up with a splitting headache, probably due to the fall from earlier, I find myself alone in the sleeping quarters and thank my lucky stars that I am still alive. I'm surprised Susie left me alone in here knowing that there is a killer on board.

Gingerly, I get up, being careful not to hit my head again on the bunk above. The room is eerily dark and still. As the blood rushes to my head the bump begins to throb.

Grateful that there aren't any glaring bright lights, I make my way into the corridor and back toward the living area where I hope that the rest of them are gathered.

Still feeling dizzy, I have to steady myself now and again and stop for short breaks. The fall wasn't that bad. Why do I feel so woozy?

As I turn a corner I almost collide with Luke who is standing in the corridor alone, looking into space.

'Hey.' Speaking hurts my brain. 'You okay?'

A strange smile works its way across his mouth and he says nothing.

'Are you all right?' I ask him.

He looks me directly in the eye but it feels as if he doesn't see me and he walks right past me, going in the direction from which I've just come.

'Luke?' I call, his name echoing around the shell of the corridor, but he keeps going.

My brief encounter with him has left me feeling more uneasy than when I woke up and so I quicken my steps, willing myself to get to the others faster.

In the living space I find Sam puffing on a cigarette. The smell makes me feel sick. He doesn't look up. Looking around I see Susie, dozing on a chair in the far corner next to Frank who is snoring beside her, sleeping with his head at the most peculiar angle.

'Where are Anya and Fiona?' I whisper, not wanting to disturb those who are resting.

'Gone to try and fix the sub.' Sam's voice is raw as if he's not slept for a millennium.

'I really don't think that is a good idea.' I gesture towards the cigarette that hangs out of his dry mouth.

'I don't give a fuck what you think.' He takes a long pull and then proceeds to blow the smoke directly into my face. I cough and back away.

His eyes are bloodshot and wild-looking so I decide not to challenge him again and meekly sit down on the other side of the room, cradling my pounding head and wishing the pain would go away. I don't trust Sam and I don't like being in his company.

We sit in silence for some minutes while he continues to furiously puff away. The smoke hangs in the air like a blanket, softening the look of everything around me. I feel so detached.

'They are wasting their time.' Sam finally speaks as he drops the butt of the cigarette into a cold mug of tea. 'We aren't getting out of here.'

'You don't know that.' I feel the tears welling up inside me.

'Yes, I do. If Fiona really thought it could work she would have tried it much sooner. She's just kidding herself and trying to give the rest of us some hope. If the lack of oxygen doesn't kill us then one of these people sure as shit will.'

'I disagree,' I protest, all the while suspecting he is right.

'You go ahead.' He chuckles. 'You'll see. We are all dead.'

At that moment Susie begins to stir. 'What is that smell?' she asks, yawning and wiping the sleep from her eyes.

'Sam thought it was a good idea to smoke,' I tell her, looking directly at him with contempt.

'What? Why would you do that?' Susie is now wide wake.

'Because I felt like it and since we are all going to die in this fucking tin can I thought I'd enjoy one last cigarette.'

There has been a change in Sam. He is more aggressive all of a sudden. I hadn't thought he had it in him when we'd first met.

'It stinks. You're selfish. I can't believe how selfish you are being.' Susie puts her sleeve up to her nose to filter the scent.

'That's not the only thing,' Sam smirks.

'What's that meant to mean?' I felt my anger beginning to build.

'Dominique,' Sam said, the word full of sadness. 'Haven't you noticed?'

In all honesty I hadn't. The only thing I could smell was the cigarette smoke, and suddenly I am grateful for that, but when he mentions the other smell it becomes the only thing I notice.

Looking over at Susie I observe the dark bags beneath her sunken eyes. She appears to have aged twenty years in just a few days.

'It's not right, her being left there. Why does nobody care?'

'I know.' I agree with Susie, sharing her sorrow. 'We should move her.'

Just then Frank opens one eye and looks around the room. I begin to suspect he hasn't been asleep at all.

'Well, I'm not moving her, doll.' He sits forward, fully alert.

'Of course not,' Sam spits. 'The great Frank Holden would never get his hands dirty, would he.'

'Watch your mouth, kid.' Frank's small eyes are full of rage.

'Whatever.' Sam shrugs, getting up and sauntering over to the coffee machine. 'Anyone want a cup?'

The thought of coffee makes me feel quite sick and I shake my head. Frank stands up and stretches out his arms, his fat gut looking more rotund than ever.

'Black with two sugars,' he says cracking his knuckles, making Susie wince at the sound.

'I wasn't talking to you,' Sam replies, making himself a cup.

In an unexpected move, Frank leaps across the room and grabs Sam by the scruff of his neck.

'Now listen to me, you little faggot. As long as there is still air in your lungs you'll remember who is in charge. Got it? You might have killed that poor fucking girl but you don't frighten me.'

Susie and I remain in our seats, powerless to interfere.

Seconds later Sam is laughing hysterically and Frank, who is confused by the reaction, lets go, stepping back and looking at Sam as if he's gone mad.

'What the hell is so funny?' Frank asks, looking less certain of himself. But Sam doesn't answer and just keeps laughing.

'Now he's lost his fucking mind too.' Frank spins round to face Susie, looking for confirmation. As he does, Sam suddenly straightens and hurls the mug of hot coffee at Frank.

It all plays out in slow motion.

The white plastic cup bounces off of Frank's egg-shaped balding head and dark, steaming coffee splashes against his skin and clothes, splattering against the walls and ceiling before the mug drops to the ground and rolls underneath the table.

As his face fills with as much shock as pain, Frank turns around to look at his attacker.

By this point I am standing and decide I need to leave the room. The atmosphere is too much to bear and the irate men are frightening me.

Scrabbling for the door I stumble into the corridor and start to yell for help. I can hear Susie a few steps behind me as the distance between my body and the fighting extends.

When I am certain we are far enough away from Sam and Frank, I stop to catch my breath. Getting away from them has taken all my strength and I sink to my knees, trying to fight the dizziness I feel.

Susie slips to the ground next to me and rests her head on my shoulder. I can feel she is shaking. We are both scared.

'He's really lost it,' Susie whispers. 'What if one of them is the one killing people on board?'

'That was scary.'

'What are we going to do?' I can hear the helplessness in her voice and wish I were strong enough to be able to offer some comfort. But I can't. I'm too weak and an emotional wreck myself.

'I saw Luke earlier,' I admit, 'and he had the weirdest look in his eye.'

'We can't stay here with these madmen.'

'What choice do we have?' The situation is hopeless.'

'We need to go find Fiona and Anya. Power in numbers.' Susie is beginning to think straight.

'Okay.' I hear the word leave my mouth but it sounds foreign.

'Come on.' Susie stands up and tries to pull me off the ground. 'We need to get moving.'

In contrast to my weakness, I am impressed with her sudden surge of strength. She doesn't look like she could hold her own but she has been a rock throughout this nightmare and I wonder how I would have coped without her.

'You're right. Fiona and Anya. We must find them.' I get to my feet and try to ignore the flood of nausea. 'Let's go.'

Child

*M*ummy had no idea Nick was coming into my room most nights to give me those special hugs, and I remembered what he'd said about not telling anyone, so I didn't. But I didn't like the hugs at all. Not one bit and I wished that he hadn't come into our lives. I would swap his attention for Mummy's anger if I could.

The funny thing that did happen was that the noise from Mummy's room stopped happening so often and, as a result, she returned to being cross most of the time, like before.

To keep myself away from the house I would I walk for hours sometimes, never knowing where I was headed. The temperature and the weather didn't affect me. I didn't mind the cold. I just put one foot in front of the other until I had quietened the rage inside. Sometimes I would walk from dusk until dawn, in the holidays, but I always found my way back home.

During that autumn I spent much of my time wandering across the fields around the outskirts of my village. I felt like a stranger in my home and to my mummy.

When I was that age, I used to wish I had a sibling. Now I am grateful I did not. Being alone taught me so much about myself and made me stronger.

School was awful. I hated every minute of it. I spent my nights crying into my blanket, trying not to let Mummy hear my sobs. She would have been so disappointed.

The teachers were strict and unapproachable. No one bothered to take the time to understand me.

The buildings were old and crumbling. The main building was built of red brick and had tall windows. The thought of it still *daunts me. Standing beneath the vast imposing structure made me feel extremely small and vulnerable. I suppose I was. To an eleven-year-old it was intimidating, which I now realise was meant to be. The buildings themselves demanded respect. There was no running, no shouting and no disobedience.*

I was easily bored and I was lonely. None of the others liked me and I was bullied year after year until I was old enough to leave.

The older children would corner me and beat me as I cowered beneath my coat for protection. Often, I would discover dead worms on my desk and once they left poo in my locker. The smell lingered for weeks. But I didn't complain. You didn't tell tales and I couldn't rely on Mummy to help me. I just had to accept it and do my best.

Sometimes after a beating I would end up wetting the bed. That only added to my problems. Mummy would scold me for being so revolting and as my confidence retreated, the other children continued their barrage of cruelty.

Having Nick come into our lives made things so much worse and I felt angry with Mummy about it.

One Christmas, when I was eleven, I asked Mummy if I could go to a different school. She told me to go to my bedroom and refused to discuss it. I did what I was told, just like I always did, and it was never mentioned again. In the New Year I was back at that school and as miserable as ever.

Apart from the bullies and the buildings, the other thing that stands out for me in my memory is the food. At best it was inedible. The worst thing was that the lunch monitors took great pleasure in forcing us to finish every last mouthful. Some of the children had gotten wise to this and would sneak in tissues in which they would wrap up their food and smuggle it out, dropping it in a bin where it belonged. I was always too frightened to do this. Getting caught would mean real trouble.

One child was beaten so badly one day after school when he didn't finish his food, that he ended up limping for a week. He took a twisted pleasure in showing us all the cuts across the back of his legs. The stick the older kids had used had cut deep into his flesh, slicing his young, white skin like butter. I remember telling him to put some cream on it. The boy pushed me over and said he'd rather be beaten again than accept any help from me. All the children standing around us laughed. I did not.

During one spring my existence was made even more miserable.

Queuing up to get my lunch, I felt my heart sink as the dinner lady plopped a faggot onto my plate. Thankfully, this food is now out of fashion. Faggots are disgusting. They are large balls of meat, often made from pigs' hearts, other offal and fatty meat, which have been minced together with breadcrumbs. No child should ever be expected to eat one. I think even a dog would turn it down.

There are times in life when you feel, in your bones, that something is brewing and that something important is about to happen. That was one of those days. Every day was the same dull, repetitive nightmare. At first, that lunchtime was no different.

So, I queued and waited for the food to be put on my plate just as all the other children did. As the slimy meat flopped onto my plate I felt my stomach hit the floor.

Trying not to look at the grey mass that rolled about on my plate, I managed to locate an empty seat in the lunch hall and sat down. It was the table that always housed the misfits. The strange ginger-haired girl, the Jewish child, the teacher's relative and me. We never spoke to each other. There was nothing to say. But we knew that we were all outcasts and this was our table. That knowledge stopped me from feeling so isolated.

I did my best to stop myself from looking directly at the misshapen ball of dog food that sat on my plate. I realised, as soon as I allowed my eyes to rest on it, that the vomit would come. It was bubbling before I even entered the food hall.

As the lunch hall emptied I felt the pressure building. The Jewish child had an out. The ginger girl managed to hide most of her lunch in a napkin that she smuggled in and the teacher's pet disappeared while I remained stuck to my seat not looking at this alien food, refusing to let it pass my lips.

It was then that one of the prefects arrived and decided to have her fun.

'Eat'. She stood over me, a big girl, nearly six feet tall, with wide calves and frizzy hair.

I stared up at her pretending to be foreign, pretending not to understand.

Her large flat leather school shoes banged down on the floor, echoing around the room.

'I said, "Eat".' The few remaining pupils put their forks down and watched with their mouths open. The monster girl ignored them and continued to focus her anger and hatred on me.

'Eat,' she bellowed for a third time.

I just remember noticing the fine layer of hair she had on her cheeks. The golden-brown hairs coated her face and I was reminded of apes and how most of us had evolved.

The angrier she got the more the hairs on her face glowed like a halo.

Have you ever seen a piece of pork that came straight from the butcher? It has hair, fine, silky hair, sticking out of its skin. Well, that is what her cheeks made me think of. Pigs. Meat.

So the girl with the hairy face, fuzzy hair and bad breath, stood over me trying to intimidate me. If size had been the deciding factor, then she would have won. Even I expected to walk away the loser in this battle, but life has a funny way of throwing up surprises.

'No.' I sat back in my chair, folded my arms and stared back at her. 'No. I won't eat that.'

Then the bully did what bullies do.

The angry pubescent girl took hold of me by the back of my head and pushed my mouth towards the faggots.

She was too young to be a coffee drinker but I remember her breath, earthy and stale as she spat into my ear. 'You will take a bite out of this or I will take a bite out of you.'

Surprisingly, I did what she requested. The mouthful of cold, rubbery, fatty, salty, meat hit my taste buds and instantly clashed.

Before I could warn her, the mixture of my porridge from breakfast and the curdled meat met in my throat and erupted all over the lunch hall, spraying everything in my path.

Yes, I did throw up all over the bully. Yes, I did stand my ground for once but it didn't do me any good. I was shoved out of the lunch hall by one of the teachers; vomit dripping from my chin, the stench on my uniform. I was then marched to the head's office, the wet, lumpy, sick still clinging to me, as I sat there waiting to receive my punishment.

I returned home late that night, because I had to spend time writing lines when everyone else was allowed to go home. Mummy didn't notice I was late but she did notice my filthy uniform and the smell. So not only had I had a horrible day at school but I was then told by Mummy that she wouldn't pay for another uniform so I'd better do a good job of cleaning it up myself.

I used water from the kettle and lots of washing-up liquid but never did manage to completely get rid of the smell.

When Nick came into my room that night I just lay there, as the tears rolled down my cheeks, and I didn't say a word.

The Pica Explorer

Day three. Hour 17:00.

'Where are they?' Susie and I had searched one end of the vessel but there was no sign of either Fiona or Anya.

'Maybe they went back to the living area. Or maybe they are dead.'

'No.' Susie shakes her head. 'We would have passed them.'

We both stand there, cold and afraid, wondering what to do next.

'I need the loo.' Susie shifts on the spot.

'Okay. Let's go back to the sleeping quarters. There is a loo there.' As we walk slowly, clinging to each other, the blue lights above our heads begin to flicker again and we quicken our pace, wary that one of the men could appear at any moment.

'I don't like this,' I whisper.

'Neither do I.' Susie squeezes my hand.

As we enter the bunkroom we discover Luke sitting bolt upright on one of the beds, looking into space. He does not acknowledge us when we come in.

'Luke?' Susie and I remain in the doorway frightened by the blank, ghostlike expression on his face.

He turns his head to look at us slowly as a demented smile creeps across his face. '*Row, row, row your boat, gently down the stream. Merrily, merrily, merrily, merrily, life is but a dream.*' His eyes are wide and staring. Then he begins again. '*Row, row, row…*'

'He's gone mad.' Susie steps backwards, keeping hold of my arm and making sure that I back away with her as his singing grows louder.

In the corridor once again Susie pulls the door closed behind her, shutting Luke alone in the room.

'Quick, look for something to secure the door,' she says frantically, keeping hold of the handle as I scrabble about looking for anything that will do the job. From the other side of the door we can still hear Luke singing the song over and over again.

As I search high and low for something that could be used to keep the door propped shut, I try to fight the daze in my head and the pounding ache from the bump on my skull.

I know Luke could get up at any moment and try to get out. There is no way on earth that Susie could possibly hold him off.

Just then Frank appears. 'What the hell are you doing?' He is panting and sweaty.

'Where is Sam?' I look at Susie, not sure that we want to know the answer.

'I gave the kid a slap. He's feeling sorry for himself but he'll be fine.' Frank's eyes sparkle with enjoyment. 'I'll ask you again: what the hell are you doing?'

'Luke is in there. He's lost it. He's really lost it. I don't think he's safe for us to be around. I think it could be him.' Susie's grip remains firmly on the door handle and I see her knuckles are beginning to turn white. 'Listen.' She cocks her head towards the door and Frank moves in closer to get a better listen.

'Is he singing?' Frank looks bemused.

'It's not funny,' I say through gritted teeth. 'He's really not well.'

'And you think that you can keep him in there, do you, doll? For all we know he is the killer, as Susie said.' Frank chuckles, running his eyes up and down Susie.

'Do you want to try instead?' she responds coldly, still entertaining the thought that Luke is the one responsible.

'Move over!' Frank barges her out of the way and wraps his large hands around the handle.

For a moment my heart is in my mouth and I think Frank is going to open the door but after a moment more of listening to Luke sing, he holds firm and the smile fades from his face.

'There is rope down in the engine room. Get it,' he barks at me, slipping back into director mode.

'No.' Susie puts her hand up taking control. 'Zara can stay here. I'll get it.' She winks at me as she rushes off to get the rope, leaving me alone with Frank.

'You shouldn't go alone, Susie,' I plead as she disappears. 'Is Sam really all right?' I ask Frank as I slide to the floor feeling dizzy.

'He's fine, doll. Go check if you like.'

Shaking my head I carefully take one hand up to feel the lump on the side of my head. It is tender to touch and I wince.

'That looks nasty,' Frank says, managing to almost sound sympathetic.

'It hurts like a bitch.' Getting to my feet I steady myself, determined to go and check that Sam is actually all right. As I do, the singing from the bunkroom grows louder still and my eyes meet Frank's.

'Fucking fruit cake.' Frank hangs his head with disappointment just as Sam comes stumbling in.

'See,' Frank says looking up, 'told you the little scrote was okay.'

'Is that Luke?' Sam's cheek is red and his jaw looks swollen. He cannot bring himself to look at Frank.

'Yes.' I nod, relieved to see that Sam has survived his encounter with Frank.

'Did they manage to fix the battery?' he asks me, trying to ignore the maniacal sound of the nursery rhyme coming from next door.

'We couldn't find them. They've vanished.'

'What?' Frank growls.

'While the two of you were tearing strips off each other, Susie and I went to try and find Fiona and Anya but they've disappeared.'

'Don't be stupid,' Frank spits. 'There is no way off of this thing.'

I don't have the energy to try and convince him that there is no sign of them and shrug instead.

'Kid, come and hold this door. I'm going to get the rope myself and find those bloody women.'

'No,' Sam refuses, looking smug. 'You're the big man. You hold the fucking door yourself.'

I watch the rage starting to rise in Frank again and wish these two men would just stop fighting for one moment but before I can say anything, a sound comes rippling up through the sub and we feel it begin to tip.

Child

*S*ome things you never forget, like your first kiss or the first time you taste alcohol.

During the summer of 1999 I spent much of the holidays roaming around the countryside. I'd go for long walks, often staying out until dusk. I was happy as long as I was away from the house and Mummy.

Nick had moved in with us but he and Mummy weren't getting on very well. He still paid regular visits to my bedroom at night while she lay sleeping.

The best thing about where we lived was that I had lots of fields around to explore. Our cottage was at the end of a small village in the countryside.

Our neighbours, Percy Barker and his wife Glenda, lived in small cottage at the end of our lane. The couple were both in their late seventies and he still worked as a gardener, mowing the lawns for the big houses in the posh villages around us. I got to know them both that year. The Barkers were always very good to me.

Glenda used to slip me bits of cake and Percy would walk me around his plot showing me the vegetables that were growing. I'd always had a fascination with nature and when I was with them I could forget about all my worries.

Percy took pride in showing me the carrots he'd grown. I remember his old gnarled hands reached into the earth and pulled up a carrot. Lovingly he wiped the dirt from it on his trousers and offered it to me. 'There you are, pet.' His voice was as soft as his soul.

Unusually, Glenda went first. After her stroke she was bedbound. A year later she died. Only a few months after that Percy followed her. He gave up living after Glenda died and soon got his wish to *be reunited with his love. I thought of them as grandparents and missed them terribly.*

I'd packed my rucksack with a cheese sandwich and a flask of water and was spending the day down by the stream among old chestnut trees that grew by the water.

On that hot spring day I found a tiny bird that had fallen from its nest. Frozen, I stood there for a moment looking at the creature, holding my breath and wondering if it was dead. Moments later it opened its small beak and let out a noise. It is a sound I will never forget.

Letting my bag drop to the ground I crouched down on my knees, a few feet away from the baby bird. I could tell it was young because some of its feathers had yet to grow. The little black-eyed bird kept squawking and opening its mouth. It was clearly hungry.

So as not to scare it, I removed the box that had my sandwiches in and opened it. The frantic creature was screaming at me by then, flapping its wings, which weren't yet properly formed.

'It's okay,' I said in a soothing voice as I tore a tiny crumb of crust from my bread, 'here you go.' Reaching over I placed the morsel into its open beak and watched the bird swallow. Less than a second later it was begging for more so I repeated the action. This went on for a little while until the bird calmed down, content and full at last. Removing the flask I then poured a little of the water onto my hands and let the drops roll of my fingers and into its mouth before sitting back and admiring my new companion.

'Where did you come from then?' I asked the now docile creature. 'You can be my new friend,' I told the chick who was squawking again. Carefully I picked it up and cradled it in the palm of my hand. It weighed almost nothing. To my surprise the bird was not alarmed by the contact and settled quickly into a comfortable position.

Standing up I went in search for its nest, looking for a sign of its parents. Up in the branches I could see a semi-collapsed nest. There was no evidence of any more chicks or the parents. This little one was completely alone. Just like me.

While deciding what to do, I slipped the bird into my cardigan pocket, sat down again and ate my sandwich.

By the time I finished my lunch I'd concocted a plan. Before I did anything else I needed to work out what kind of bird it was. It wasn't easy to tell just by looking at the few dirty brown feathers that covered its small pink body. I knew that in the school library there would be a book that would answer my question so I gathered my flask and bag from the ground and set off in the direction of home, whistling as I went. I was so excited. I'd never had a pet before.

It took me thirty minutes to get back home as I walked very slowly with the bird in my pocket, taking care not to squash it.

I didn't know where Mummy and Nick were so I tiptoed through the house not wanting to attract any attention. My beige socks had a hole in, which one of my small white toes poked out through. I held my breath, making sure I didn't make any sound but at that moment my little companion decided to perk up and started calling for more food. Terror gripped me as I put my hand over the bird and rushed into my bedroom hoping that no one was at home and had heard.

Once in my room, I closed the door, leant against it and let out a sigh. Then I listened for footsteps and only when I was certain that no one was there did I allow myself to make myself at home on my bed while the little bird cried for more food.

Realising I needed something to house the bird in, I looked for something suitable under my bed.

Right at the back, behind some old clothes, I discovered an empty shoebox. It would make a perfect home for my friend until it learnt how to fly.

Using a pencil that was lying on the table by my bed, I poked some holes into the lid so that I could be sure the bird would be able to breathe once inside. Then I put it carefully into the box. The bird settled quickly but I felt sad looking at it alone in that vast cardboard space. It may not have resembled a nest but I knew the bird would at least be safe in there. It could not fall out. From another pocket I took out a small crust of bread that I had saved and broke a small piece off, dropping it into the tiny beak, repeating this until the bird stopped crying again. I smiled at the content bird. At last I had something in my life that was good.

The spring sunlight poured in onto the faded curtain that I pushed back, before hiding the bird on the indoor sill and replacing the curtain. I knew that the trapped sun would help to keep the bird warm.

I managed to keep it there undiscovered for some days, before the holidays came to an end. The only good thing about going back to school was that I could get access to the library and the many reference books.

During my lunch break, while the other children were outside playing, I went to the library. Some of the books looked really old and dusty. Methodically I started on the left-hand wall, at the bottom and worked my way up. A few times I was distracted by other books but I was not sure how long I had left in there before someone found me so I decided to keep focused.

The first helpful book I come across was an encyclopaedia of British birds. It had lovely hand illustrated pictures of each species and it didn't take me too long to identify my friend. Although I couldn't be certain, because the feathers were not fully developed yet, I hazarded a guess that it was a baby sparrow. I also learnt that such birds are mainly seedeaters, so felt relieved that feeding it the bread wasn't too bad.

As I lost myself in the book, absorbing as much information as I could, I heard a noise from the corridor outside. Closing the book I put it back on the shelf, making a mental note of where I left it. When I was sure that the coast was clear I snuck out of the library and made my way to the playground.

I knew then that the little bird needed my help otherwise it would die and I made a promise to myself to do everything I could to help it survive.

Once back at home and in my bedroom I said hello to my little friend, who I had managed to keep a secret. Mummy would have never let me keep an animal in the house.

Kneeling on the floor I removed the paper in my pocket, which I took from school, and started to tear it into strips. I loved the noise of paper tearing, especially when done slowly.

When all the sheets had been shredded I arranged the paper on the floor of the box for the bird, which sat in the corner blinking at me while I worked.

'This is to make it comfortable for you,' I explained wondering if the sparrow was male or female. The book taught me that it was almost impossible to tell.

When the paper had been layered into a nest-like shape, I sat looking down at the bird wondered if maybe I could somehow get a sense of the sex.

'What are you?' I asked it, examining the features. 'I think you need a name. I am going to call you Robin.'

***

After Robin came into my life I found myself watching any bird that crossed my path. I became obsessed with learning everything I could about them. In my spare time, and at night, I would read books about birds from all over the world, studying their biology, history and habits. In those days it wasn't as easy to access information. Not like it is now with computers, iPhones and Google. Those were different times. But thanks to the extensive library in town, I had a large selection of books at my fingertips.

Apart from research I also started to draw birds. I'd spend many hours sitting in my room watching Robin and making sketches. My early drawings were not good but as the weeks passed I began to get better. When I wasn't sketching Robin I'd copy drawings of other birds out of the books I kept hidden underneath my bed.

All the time there was an impending sense of doom, which I did my best to ignore but as August came to an end I had to face up to the inevitable; soon I would be returning to school. The thought of being there, away from Robin, made me feel sick. I hated that place. I had no friends but at home I had the best friend a child could ever wish for. Robin was my special friend and taught me I didn't need people.

Luke

Leaving the countryside was easy. I never much liked the place. I had a few buddies but no one special to keep me there. So when a bit of inheritance came my way I packed a bag and left for London. My dad hadn't been around and my mum, well, let's just say we didn't get on very well.

I did okay in school. Not very academic, is how people probably described me. I liked art and sport but wasn't very good at putting pen to paper and my maths skills were non-existent.

I was a skilled cameraman but self-taught. No posh film school for me. I wouldn't have fitted in anyway. I'm more the type who likes to learn by practising. Never could be told anything.

I started off doing weddings. Pretty boring but it paid the bills and I got to understand about lighting and the things that have an effect on what it is you are shooting. Besides, following pretty bridesmaids round wasn't so bad.

It was at a wedding that I met Jürgen. He was in the business and we got chatting about cameras. He liked the equipment I was using and was impressed by my knowledge of the kit.

After he'd had a few glasses of bubbly he gave me his card and told me to get in touch if I ever wanted to do something other than film weddings. The next Monday I was on the phone to him. In all honesty, I wasn't sure he'd remember me but he did and we arranged to meet for a talk.

Jürgen was typically German. Sandy-haired, quite tall, could hold his drink and had a sense of humour. I liked him from the get-go and he seemed to like me. Like lots of people in the film world, he'd started off in advertising. He told me stories about his career and the people he'd met and worked with, including Frank Holden. I was young and easily impressed.

Jürgen told me I reminded him of himself when he was younger. He said he could see I had talent and wanted to help me get my big break. He offered me work alongside him. He had plenty of projects on the go and said he needed a bright and reliable cameraman. Apparently I was it.

When I first stepped on set with him I was shitting myself. Everyone there seemed so suave and sure of themselves and there I was, a working class boy with no experience. I felt right out of my depth. But soon I learnt the ropes and started to get good at my job.

After working on a few mini-series with Jürgen, I was in for a meeting with him. He has an office in a building on Cross Keys Close, in Marylebone, just off Thayler Street. The building is one of those old flat-fronted Victorian places you often see in London side streets. He is on the second floor and his office space only occupies a couple of rooms. It's decked out with lots of mid-century Danish furniture that is really popular with trendy, arty London types. I don't like it much.

I sat down by the coffee table and he offered me a drink.

'We have a really cool coffee machine. Would you like an espresso?' Jürgen sat cross-legged, sipping piping hot coffee from a small glass coffee cup.

'No thanks, mate. Not much of a coffee drinker.'

I was still finding my feet in the film world. They had a way of doing things that was alien to the likes of me. The people I'd grown up with drank good old English tea. None of this foreign coffee that was so popular in London.

'No problem.' Jürgen put his cup down. 'I have a job coming up that I think you might be interested in.' Jürgen's blue eyes danced with excitement. 'But you gotta keep it real hush hush and low down.'

'Lips are sealed.' I leant forward, mimicking his body language.

'A really exciting opportunity. This could be huge. Really big.' Jürgen rubbed his hands together. 'I told you I knew Frank Holden, well he's been talking to me about a film he wants to make. He wants me involved in the planning of the movie. I told him I was interested and I told him about this great guy I work with.' Then he paused. 'You.'

I couldn't believe Jürgen had spoken to the mighty Frank Holden about me.

'It's a real secret at the moment. Frank doesn't want the press getting any wind about it.' Jürgen's grasp on the English language occasionally left something to be desired. 'He has commissioned a submarine. The action takes place underwater.'

'Sounds like a challenge.' I ran my hand though my hair, ruffling it up. I needed a moment to take everything in.

'Sure, but that is what Frank is all about: challenges. He likes to do things differently. He like to move the boundaries.'

'I've seen some of his films.'

'Then you know what it is I am talking about.' Jürgen clasped his hands together. 'This is a good starting point.' He took another sip of his espresso. 'So, I told Frank I would be involved but that I would not want to go on the submarine. I don't like confined spaces. He understood and said this wasn't a problem.' It was hard to imagine that Jürgen was frightened of anything. 'So, Luke, I spoke to Frank in more detail and I think this is a really exciting opportunity for a man at your stage in his career. The question I have for you is, are you interested in this job?' He adjusted his glasses with his right hand, which he always did when he was being very serious, and leant back in his chair. 'You have the talent. Now is the question: do you have the balls?'

I'd heard rumours about Frank Holden. You would have to have been deaf to miss them. But the rumours were about his fondness for young female actresses so I knew I wasn't in any danger of unwelcome advances.

'What's the money like?' I was hoping the film came with a large budget.

'Ha!' Jürgen leant forward and slapped my shoulders. 'This is a very good question to ask.' I grinned, waiting for his response. 'This isn't as big a budget as some of the other films he has made but I am told by him that the money is good.'

That wasn't quite the answer I was hoping for.

'So how long will we be shooting for?'

'I have a meeting with Frank to talk about this some more. But I wanted to feel you out first.' I stifled a smile.

'Okay. I am interested. Of course I bloody am. I'd be mental to turn down a chance to work with the big man himself.' I still couldn't quite believe it. 'Count me in.'

***

I went home and opened my Mac laptop. I wanted to know more about Frank Holden and soon discovered he'd been dropped from a blockbuster series, that one with the incestuous wizard, and hadn't worked for some time. It was clear that something had happened to change his fortune. Big players like Frank don't just suddenly stop producing stuff. But I couldn't see how that played a part in this new film. Everyone has a past, don't they.

After Googling Frank, I then went on to do some research about submarines. I'd never been on one before and the idea of it was exciting but it left me feeling uncertain. How long would we be on it for? How many of us would be on board? Jürgen had given me hardly any information to go on.

But I suppose the mystery also made it seem like more of an adventure. I couldn't believe how much my life had changed since I'd left the countryside. My childhood was now a distant memory and for that I was grateful.

That night, to celebrate the job, I went and got some beers from the shop down the road. I downloaded Frank's best-known film and drank all six tins of Stella while watching it.

At one point my housemate came in and sat with me. The film was violent and full of action. Frank sure knew how to tell a story using the camera.

I concentrated hard and it gave me a clue as to how Frank liked to work. I had a feeling I was about to be dropped in the deep end with this one.

I'd met Bowzer, one of my flatmates, whose real name was Robbie, through an ad. He and a couple of other lads had been flat-sharing and needed someone to fill the extra room. I moved in a few days later.

The place wasn't exactly a palace but it was quite central and near a Tube so it ticked enough boxes.

Bowzer sat down next to me, stuffing his face with a kebab. He was spilling the filling everywhere. Chilli sauce ended up on the sofa, as well as bits of gherkin and wet lettuce.

'Come on, man! You eat like a pig.' I dodged a mouthful of doner meat that had fallen on the sofa next to me.

Bowzer grinned, showing me a mouthful of food.

'You're a bloody animal,' I told him, picking up a cushion and whacking him around the face with it.

'Oi.' Bowzer looked genuinely upset.

'Sorry, bro, but I'm trying to watch this.' I wiped the remnants of food from the cushion. 'Can I let you into a little secret?' I could feel the beer beginning to have the desired effect.

'Sure thing.' Bowzer continued munching on his food, which by then must have been stone cold.

'I've landed a gig working with... drum roll please... Frank Holden.'

'No way!' Bowzer's eyes widened in disbelief.

'I shit you not. But you gotta keep this to yourself.' I winked at him.

'You're full of it,' Bowzer continued speaking despite his mouthful.

'No, I'm not. Had a meeting with the German fella I work with today and he told me he put me forward to work on Frank's next film.' I smiled with pride.

'You're gonna be, like, famous.' He sunk into the sofa and stared at the scene for a bit. 'You'll have your name in the credits and stuff when the film ends. That will be awesome.' It became quickly apparent that Bowzer had smoked a few joints that night.

After he'd devoured his kebab we stayed up chatting about films. Bowzer rolled himself a joint and we decided to watch another Frank Holden flick.

Thanks to the beers I fell asleep halfway through the film, which I'd seen a few times before. Soon I was in a deep and restless sleep, tormented by a recurring nightmare, which had plagued me for years. My childhood hadn't been easy.

I woke up on the sofa the next morning dripping in sweat and breathless. Bowzer lay next to me with his hood pulled up, snoring like a dog. The place still smelt of kebab and the room was a mess of beer cans and trainers. Remembering the events from the day before, it occurred to me that I would enjoy being away from the flat for a while. The lads were all nice enough but I didn't want to live in a dump anymore. I wanted more out of life.

Leaving Bowzer still sleeping, I slowly started to collect the empty cans and dirty food wrappers to put in the rubbish. The feeling from the nightmare still lingered and I felt out of sorts for the rest of the day.

The Pica Explorer

Day three. Hour 17:15.

Grabbing hold of anything sturdy, we brace ourselves as the sub begins to tip slowly onto one side.

'What is happening?' Frank's face is filled with horror.

I close my eyes and try to imagine myself anywhere other than where I am while my stomach begins to churn like a washing machine.

But then, as quickly as it started, it stops. I open my eyes, still clinging to the pipes, to see Frank and Sam's pale faces. We haven't tipped as much as I thought.

'What the fuck was that?' Sam fumbles in his pocket, and I worry he is going to pull out a weapon, but I see his hands shaking as he tries to remove a packet of cigarettes and I feel instant relief.

Frank straightens and tries to regain his composure but it is clear he is just as spooked as the rest of us. Thankfully his grip remains firm on the door handle, keeping Luke at bay.

The singing has stopped.

'Where is that girl with the rope?' I think it is odd that Frank calls Susie a girl, considering she is in her mid-forties, but I realise it is just another method he uses to belittle.

'I'll go and make sure she is okay,' I say, finally finding the courage to let go of the pipe I was clinging to for support. 'It's not safe for her to be walking around here alone.'

'What if it starts to tip again?' Sam still hasn't been able to remove the cigarettes from his pocket.

'Hold on, arsehole,' Frank growls.

'I think I'll come with you.' Sam curls his lip at Frank before turning to me.

But can I trust Sam?

Without warning, a scream comes rattling through the corridor, bouncing off the metal walls like a ball. We fall quiet and all turn in the direction it came from. Then there is nothing but silence.

Above us the blue lights blink and the faint buzzing of electricity can be heard passing above our heads. For a moment we are plunged into darkness and I think to myself, *this is it*. But just when I am about to give up hope, the lights flicker back on again.

'Maybe we should stay put,' Sam says still staring up at the ceiling.

'The scream.' I point in the direction the sound came from.

'Maybe it was the darkness that made them scream?' Sam knows it came from one of the women at the other end of the submarine.

'We have to go and find out.' I am feeling so weak, it is as if I am floating on a cloud above and watching this all play out. 'It might be Susie.' She is all I can think about.

'Go,' Frank orders in his director's tone of voice. 'Find out what is going on and bring me that goddamn rope.'

Sam, who I am expecting to refuse, nods his head and beckons for me to come.

Despite feeling lightheaded, I manage to put one foot in front of the other and slowly make my way along the narrow corridor, following Sam cautiously towards the back of the sub. A moment or two later we are outside the periscope room, which we need to pass through. Strangely the door is shut. I try the handle but I am too weak. Huffing with frustration Sam then has a go. The door opens with ease.

There we discover Susie standing holding the rope she'd been sent to retrieve. She looks at us and points toward the ladder with a quivering hand.

Fiona is strung up by her neck; dead. Her eyes are swollen and bloodshot and a small amount of blood has gathered in the corner of her mouth. Her head hangs to one side and the noose cuts into the skin around her throat.

It takes a moment for it all to sink in but then I notice that her hands are bound together behind her back.

'Jesus, fuck.' Sam takes a step back, cracking his elbow against the wall.

Susie remains glued to the spot and is shaking like a leaf. I reach out to touch her but she recoils, her eyes wide and fearful.

'It's me,' I say gently, wanting to give her a hug, as much for my sake as for hers.

'We have to get her down.' Susie finally manages to speak but her words are distant. 'We can't leave her tied there.' It seems that all of the emotional strength she had has now been shattered.

Sam doesn't move. I look back up at the corpse, which looks more like a plastic prop than a person.

'This is like a horror film,' I say.

'You.' Susie's eyes start to fill with tears. 'You are going to get her down now.' She moves towards Sam, pointing a slender finger at his face. 'Now.' Suddenly there is no more fear, only anger.

Sam hangs his head in shame and then agrees to her demands. 'You can see the ropes are tied tight.'

'So use your strength.' Suddenly I remember why Susie is a good producer. She may appear petite and harmless but beneath the surface is a strong woman.

Tentatively, Sam approaches the ladder and begins to fumble with the ropes that are cutting into Fiona's flesh. He has to use one hand to push her body to the side so that he can continue to access the ropes unobstructed by her lifeless body.

Watching Sam struggle to untie the cord that is wrapped around Fiona's neck, I can't help but feel pity for him. He is a young man who got on this submarine looking for stardom. Instead, he has ended up living in a nightmare surrounded by death. Suddenly I don't suspect him anymore.

'You better move out of the way,' he says. 'When I manage to untie this she is going to fall hard.'

Susie ushers me to the side of the small room and we wait for the body to be released.

'Any minute now,' Sam warns us.

Seconds later Fiona's body flops down from her resting place and ends up slumped on the floor, her bones cracking as her lifeless body makes contact with the unforgiving surface below.

The body lands in a strange position, her legs splaying in an unnatural fashion. As Sam descends he stops a few rungs before the bottom and has to jump off the ladder and over her crumpled body.

'Now what?' He is breathing deeply, the shock settling on his face.

'I don't know who could have done this,' Susie admits, 'but I think I should get this rope to Frank and we can deal with it later.'

'Where is Anya?' Sam asks suddenly.

'I don't know. I went to retrieve the rope and on my way back I found Fiona. She must have been there for a while but I didn't notice on my way past the first time. I thought they must have both come back and found you.'

Susie fumbles with the rope in her hand, twisting it tightly around her wrists and fingers, cutting off the blood before releasing it again.

'Should we look for her? Maybe she is in trouble,' I ask while trying not to look at the contorted, broken body that lies on the floor only a few feet away.

'The rope first.' Susie holds it up. 'Then we go and find Anya.'

'Don't you realise that it was Anya who did this?' Sam looks at us as if we are stupid. 'Anya and Fiona were together. We were all together. Now Fiona is dead and Anya is missing. It wasn't me.'

As I take a moment to think about it, I do see that his logic makes sense. 'You can play detective later,' Susie snaps, 'I need to get this to Frank. There are too many mad people on board and if we can do something to contain one of them then that is what I intend to do.'

With a fierceness that has only recently become apparent, Susie marches out of the room, her head held high and her hand gripping the rope tightly. Half an hour later, Susie, Sam, Frank and I are all back in the living area, sipping tea in silence.

Luke, who has been silent ever since the submarine moved, is now securely looked in the bedroom. He has a bathroom so he can access water from the tap. He won't die of dehydration.

None of us have thought about what to do in the long term, if there is one.

'Did you all feel the submarine move?' Susie finally looks up from her tea.

'Sure did.' Frank sits there with a scowl on his face.

'What do you think it was?'

'I was hoping Fiona or Anya could answer but...' Sam's words trail off.

'It seems the batteries weren't fixed then and now it seems pretty clear that Anya is the loon.' Frank cups his mug of tea with his large hands, and sadness spreads across his face.

'Don't you think we should try to find Anya?' Susie looks to me.

I shrug. I'm finding it difficult to care about anything anymore.

'If we do, we should put her in the room with Luke.' Sam is so white his skin appears almost see-through. The short kempt beard he once kept has now become straggly. Gradually we are all giving up.

'Damn it'—Frank slams his mug down on the table spilling half the contents—'can't anyone else smell that? It stinks.'

No one says anything at first. We all know what's causing it and we can all smell it too. It's been in the air for a while and it is getting stronger.

'Well you could have helped put them in the freezer,' Sam says with spite.

'Them?' Susie's lip begins to tremble. 'You are talking about people, not pieces of meat. I can't believe this is happening.'

I can't listen to any more so I put my hands up over my ears and rock myself slowly back and forth, trying to escape from the horrifying reality.

With my eyes closed all I can see is Fiona's face in my mind; how swollen it was, how blue it went. I am going to die in this place, surrounded by bodies until the oxygen finally runs out and I take my last sad breath.

Child

I'd gotten used to living with Nick and his special hugs. It became a normal part of life although it made me feel dirty.

Mummy and Nick were arguing a lot. He wasn't working and spent lots of time at home, sitting on the sofa and watching TV.

'You're a lazy slob. Stop living off your woman. Be a man!' I used to hear Mummy say when they were shouting at each other.

During their fights, which I think were also physical, I would sneak out of the house and go into the shed, where Robin lived. I'd moved the bird in there as soon as it was fully grown. It needed room to fly. Neither Mummy or Nick ever went into the shed. It had nothing much in it apart from some very old paint pots and rusty garden tools that I'm sure they didn't know existed. It was a safe place for me to keep my secret.

Robin was always so pleased to see me that it helped me to forget what it was I was trying to escape. The bird was so tame it would fly straight onto my finger and let me stroke the soft feathers on its chest.

Every day, on my walk to school, I would keep an eye out for worms. Whenever it had rained they would appear on the path and I'd pick them up and put them into an empty matchbox. It would remain in my pocket all day until I got home when I'd rush to give my friend the treat.

I did steal some money from Mummy's purse so that I could buy Robin some birdseed. The bird didn't seem to like the worms much. It wasn't very much money but I did feel bad, although I knew other kids were given pocket money by their parents. I heard some people talk about it in the playground once. I never got pocket money. It was a miracle if I had a present from her for my birthday.

Mummy sometimes gave me some pound coins and told me to go and get myself something. Usually, I bought sweets.

That day was just like the rest. I fed and chatted to Robin before going in to make myself my tea. I sat alone at the kitchen table and ate a boiled egg and bread with butter, then had an apple.

At eight-thirty I took myself up to bed and waited for the visit from Nick, which normally came at about half-past eleven. I hated him coming into my room, the smell of kebab on his breath.

That night was no different at first. I faced the wall while Nick hugged me and stared out the window at the stars. My curtains weren't properly closed so I could see the night sky. I liked looking at it. Sometimes I used to think I was an alien who had ended up on the wrong planet. I imagined the place where I really belonged, a long way away from Nick, Mummy and school.

As I allowed myself to daydream I heard my bedroom door swing open. I turned my head to see Mummy standing there watching us. I'd seen her look at me with disgust before but the look on her face then is something I won't ever forget.

She launched forward grabbing Nick by the back of his T-shirt and pulled him off me. I rolled into a ball and pulled the covers up over my head while I listened to her scream and hit him.

'Get out! You horrible fucking man! Get out of my house!'

I listened to her tirade carry on as she followed him out onto the landing and down the stairs.

Frozen and unable to move I thought I was going to die from shame. The shouting carried on for a while and I heard things being thrown. Then the front door slammed shut and everything went quiet. After that the only noise I heard was Mummy sobbing. That went on for a while.

It was twelve-thirty when I heard her footsteps coming up the stairs. I could hear that she was walking slower than usual. Then her bedroom door closed.

As soon as I heard that sound I jumped out of bed, pulled on some trousers and tiptoed downstairs. I needed to see Robin. I needed to be with my friend.

Passing through the living room, which had a broken lamp lying on the floor, I went into the kitchen and to the back door. The key was always left in the lock so I didn't have any difficulty getting into the garden.

My feet were bare and it was cold outside but I had to get out of the house. I wanted to be close to something that loved me.

The long grass was icy and crunchy beneath my feet and I rushed down to the other end of the garden and into the shed. Robin had been sleeping and was surprised by my arrival. I called the little bird, which sat on a high plank shelf looking at me for a while before it flew down onto my finger.

'Hello, little bird.' I hadn't realised I was crying. The bird didn't like that my hand was shaking and so returned to its position on the plank.

'Don't be like that,' I sobbed, 'it's me. Please come down.' I shone the torch up. But the bird decided it wanted to go back to sleep and gradually closed its eyes.

I returned to the house with my head hung low, feeling the deepest, saddest I ever have.

The next day Mummy left for work without saying a word to me. There was a strange atmosphere in the house. As I left for school I saw a bin bag by the front door. It was filled with all of Nick's things.

The day at school went by really slowly. I just wanted to get back to Robin and the shed where I felt safe.

On the walk back it was raining but I didn't mind. I just was pleased to be away from school. Given how Mummy had behaved that morning, I wasn't sure what to expect when I got back and as I turned the corner onto our lane I was surprised to see lights on in the house. Mummy wasn't usually back from work until later and I wondered if maybe Nick had come back to the house.

As I reached the path to the front door I looked down at the weeds that were growing through the broken paving slabs. Suddenly I felt sad that I lived in a house that wasn't loved. I'd pass other houses on my walks, and notice how tidy and cared for they appeared. Our house wasn't like that.

I opened the door carefully and looked around to see if Nick was there. Although the lights in the living room were on it was empty and I felt a wave of relief. I hung my bag and coat on a peg and went into the kitchen to stand by the stove. The rain had soaked my clothes and I was shivering from the cold.

In the kitchen I found Mummy sitting alone at the table. She had a stony look on her face and I froze. Why was she home from work so early? Her eyes looked me up and down.

The rainwater was dripping off me and splashing on the tiled floor. The hatred in her eyes made me wish I had never been born. I didn't know what to do. So I just stood there looking at the small puddle of water gathering on the floor around my feet. My shoes were muddy and I knew that would upset Mummy, too.

'Sit down.' She pointed to the chair opposite her. Her hand was trembling with rage and the fear inside me made me feel sick, but I did as I was told. 'Now. You and I need to have a little chat.' Her voice was strangely soft.

I couldn't look her in the eye. The disappointment on her face was too much for me to bear.

'We need to talk about him.' She couldn't bring herself to say his name. 'He has gone and he won't be coming back.' There was a touch of sadness in her voice. 'He has left for good.' I could hear her choking back tears. 'Your little affair is over.'

It was then that I looked up.

'You thought you could sleep with my man and get away with it. I should have known, a good-for-nothing little piece of shit like you would stoop that low. Look at you, you're a disgusting little maggot. Why he fell for it I will never know. You perverted him, somehow, twisted his mind. You make me sick. I cannot believe you came out of my body. I should have gotten rid of you the moment I discovered I was pregnant. You are as worthless and revolting as your father.'

I was speechless. She had always been cruel to me but to think that I was responsible for what Nick did to me made me want to curl up and die.

'You've been keeping secrets from me for too long. You thought you were smarter than me, but you were wrong. I found out. I always find out.' A twisted smile spread across her face and she bent down to retrieve something from the ground beneath her seat. Producing a small box she put it on the table between us. I didn't know what I was supposed to do.

'You see, last night, I watched you. I watched you with him and I saw that look on your face, the enjoyment, and I thought to myself that I would be better off if you were dead. But then'—she waggled her finger in the air—'Mummy would go to prison and Mummy doesn't want to go to prison because of a little scrote like you. So I got rid of him instead.' She sat back in her chair.

'Then when I heard the backdoor open and I looked out of my window into the garden.' She was enjoying herself and her eyes shone. 'Guess what I saw in the garden late last night?'

It was then that I realised she had discovered my secret.

'Yes, that's right. I saw you, pathetic you, slithering like a worm into the shed, and I thought to myself, I wonder why this worm is heading to the shed. So, after you'd come back and gone to bed I went and had a look for myself. Guess what I found?' She shoved the box violently with one finger and I heard Robin cheep.

'That's right. I discovered the other secret you were keeping from me.'

I felt the blood drain from my face. My throat was too dry to speak and I couldn't take my eyes off the box.

'So.' She leant forward, opened the box and removed Robin carefully with one hand. 'I wonder to myself, what am I meant to do when my child starts keeping things from me?' She cupped Robin in her hands and brought the bird to her mouth, planting a small kiss on the creature's head.

'This is the bird and you are the worm. Oh the irony!' She threw her head back and cackled while I held my breath waiting for something terrible to happen.

'You must understand I can't let you get away with this treachery.' I wanted to close my eyes but I couldn't look away from Robin as

Mummy transferred the bird into one hand. Slowly, she unfolded one of the wings so that all of the feathers were fanned out. 'This is happening because of you. You are responsible for this,' she said calmly as she twisted then ripped the wing off of the bird. It cried out in agony as Mummy threw the broken wing onto the floor before turning the bird over and doing the same on the other side. Robin's black eyes looked bigger than ever and its little beak opened and closed silently and the life seeped out of the bird.

I could not move. I could not speak and I watched in frozen horror as Mummy then dropped the wingless bird onto the floor before bringing her foot down hard on top of it.

She clapped her hands together and pretended to dust them off.

'Now, worm, clean this up.'

The Pica Explorer

Day five. Hour 21:20.

W e've been down here for five days now and only six of us remain. Ten got on board but only six are still breathing.

Luke is locked in a room and Anya is missing. We have no idea where she is. We've looked but there are so many corners in this place it is difficult to know where she might be hiding. We aren't as familiar with the submarine as she is, which puts us in a vulnerable position. She must have killed Fiona but is she responsible for the other murders? It is the only explanation. But now she is out there somewhere. She has the upper hand. She is in control.

We four — me, Susie, Frank and Sam — have all agreed to spend our time together in one room, only leaving to visit the loo. But we always go in pairs. Frank and Sam, despite the tension, agreed it makes sense to stick together. We've collected all the knives and keep them on the living room table, just in case Anya appears.

It's increasingly hard to sleep. This is something we do in turns. One of us will remain awake while the others sleep. We need to be cautious and vigilant.

Now it is my turn. We all sat and ate a meal of baked beans before settling down for the night. I say 'night' but down here there is no real concept of time. No daylight exists this far down.

The men dragged some mattresses from the other bunkroom into the living area and we've made this our quarters. There is a loo close by and we have quick access to the kitchen and storeroom where the food is kept.

Once in a while one of us goes and checks on Luke. We open the door and take in bread and tea. He is still just sitting on the bunk, looking up at the ceiling. He refuses to look at any of us, but the singing has stopped, which is something. Yesterday he pleaded with Susie to let him out. I think she probably considered it but didn't want to risk endangering any of us, which was the right decision. She did say that he seemed a lot calmer and much more in touch with reality. I wonder...

I sit at the table while the rest of them lie on the mattresses. I watch them sleep. Has Anya been the one bumping everyone off or is there another explanation? When they are sleeping they have pained expressions on their faces. We can't even escape this place in our dreams.

I wonder if anyone will come and rescue us. I wonder whether there will be anyone on board left alive to rescue.

Picking at a piece of bread and jam, I struggle to stay awake. My eyelids are heavy and I long to rest my head. The wound by my eye is less sore than it was and I can see a little bit more now, but fatigue is forcing my eyes closed. Getting up I shake my head, trying to fight the sleep that is threatening to drag me under. I pace back and forth, trying to work out a way out of this nightmare. There must be a way out. There has to be something I can do to survive.

The scent in the air makes it hard to think. The dead are rotting and the smell of death hangs in the air like a fog that grows stronger with each passing day. It clogs my mind and I can't focus on any one thought for more than a few moments.

Now that I have acknowledged the smell again I can't escape it and feel sick once more. All I can do is sip on a bottle of water to fight it. I'm not sure it is helping but at least I feel as if I am doing something to combat the nausea.

Convinced that the only solution is to leave the safety of our makeshift living space, I tiptoe past the sleeping bodies and step out into the corridor where the smell is worse. But turning right, away from where the dead lie, I make my way towards the bunkroom Luke is kept in. Once outside the door I put my ear to it to see if I can hear anything. There is silence.

'Luke?' Nothing. 'Please talk to me. It's Zara.' Still nothing. 'Are you okay? I have just come to check if you need anything.' That is a lie. I've come to escape the smell of rotten flesh and because I feel frightened and alone.

On the other side of the door I hear a loud sigh. I know he is awake and listening. I whisper, 'Thank you', close my eyes and rest my forehead against the cold door.

'What are you doing?' Frank's low voice makes me jump.

'You scared the crap out of me.' I feel myself shaking.

'Why are you talking to him? Why did you leave us sleeping alone? That mad bitch could have snuck in and cut all our throats.' The skin around his eyes is dark and his face looks grey.

'I just came to check on him. That's all.'

'At the possible expense of our lives.'

'Don't be so dramatic.' I push past him and head back towards the quarters we have been living in. As I walk I hear Frank's heavy footsteps behind me. He doesn't speak.

Once back in the room I find Susie and Sam still sleeping. Moments later Frank appears. He stands over the sleeping pair and looks at them for some time before bellowing loudly.

'Wake up!' he shouts over and over again.

Susie and Sam both sit bolt upright, rubbing their eyes before looking at Frank with shock and horror.

'We're awake,' Susie says with irritation and gets to her feet.

'We can't trust her. She is the killer!' Frank swings round pointing a finger at me. 'She wants us all dead.'

'You, maybe,' Sam laughs.

'She left us all here while she went to visit Luke. When I found her she was whispering something. She cannot be trusted.'

'I just stepped out for a minute.'

'A minute is all it takes. The devil only needs a minute.'

'The devil?' Susie looks at me with pity.

'She's no devil.' Sam rolls his eyes.

'There is a devil here, on this submarine.'

Susie comes and put her arm around me for support.

'You need to calm down, Frank,' she says.

'Do you want to die?' Frank's crazed eyes search Susie's face.

'I was checking Luke was all right. That's all.'

'I'm sure. It's okay. You don't have to explain. The pressure is getting to us all.'

'Frank, you need to fucking relax.' Sam yawns and starts to make himself a cup of tea. 'No harm done.'

'There is a mad bitch on board killing people. We are living like animals at the bottom of the ocean, surrounded by dead bodies. The harm has already been done.'

'Not by me!' I start to blub, my shoulders shaking. 'I've never hurt a fly. I just wanted to talk to Luke. I'm sorry.' The tears feel cold on my cheeks. 'I didn't mean to let you down.'

'You've not let anyone down,' Susie soothes. 'We are all feeling the pressure.'

'We agreed,' Frank growls, 'that we would stick together. All she had to do was keep watch. Not exactly fucking rocket science.' He reaches over and picks up a knife.

'I'm keeping hold of this. I don't trust any of you. Not one of you. Come near me and I'll kill you. Do you understand?'

Susie and I share a look.

'You are the one who cannot be trusted,' Sam says with spite. 'You are the only devil on board.'

'Shut up, boy.' Frank turns to face Sam. 'I could gut you like a fish.'

'Come on now,' Susie pleads, 'enough is enough. We are all scared but we have to work as a team. This isn't helping.'

Frank takes a large step towards Sam, holding the large kitchen knife in his hand as Sam's eyes widen and fill with fear.

'I've had enough of your backchat,' Frank says through gritted teeth.

'He didn't mean it,' I sob, 'you didn't. Did you, Sam?' I look at him, hoping he will agree and apologise but there is a long silent pause before Sam starts clapping.

'At last, we get to see your true colours. At last you show us all who you really are. Ladies, I present to you the real Frank Holden.'

I take a step back and hold my breath as the lights start to flicker again.

'You are not welcome in this room anymore. If you want to live, you need to leave. Now. I don't care where you go but you will not set foot back in here unless you want me to drag this blade across your throat.' Frank brings the knife up to his mouth and kisses it.

'Don't do this,' Susie begs. 'We have to stay together. If you kick him out, he is as good as dead.'

'I would rather die alone than be anywhere near this monster.' Sam turns to her and smiles sadly. 'I will gladly leave.' Sam picks up a blanket from the floor, throws it over his shoulders and turns to leave. 'Good luck, ladies.'

'No.' Susie goes to him and grabs him by the arm. 'You mustn't leave.' The blue lights flicker again.

'If he stays here, I will kill him.' Frank chuckles like a madman.

Unable to move or say anything, I look at them all. It doesn't feel as if I am part of the scene, it is as if it is happening to someone else.

'Frank.' Susie's soft voice is comforting. 'You need to put the knife down. There has been enough bloodshed. This isn't you. You aren't a killer. It doesn't have to be this way.'

Sam hangs his head and shakes it slowly, as if he believes Susie is wasting her time on him.

'Come on, Frank.' Susie lets go of Sam's arm and approaches Frank. 'Give me the knife. We can all sit down and talk this through calmly.' But Frank shows no signs that he is willing to relinquish his weapon.

Susie is now very close to him. She reaches out her hand asking for the knife again. I cannot take my eyes off the blade glinting below the electric light.

'Come on, Frank. Give me the knife.' Susie edges closer still. Just then there is a crackling noise and the lights start to flicker before we are all plunged into darkness.

Unable to see in the blackness, I strain to hear. There is no sound and this time the blue lights stay off.

Child

I remember one morning, soon after Mummy killed Robin, putting on my uniform. It was not something I liked doing but something I had to do, even if I felt like a visitor, a tourist, out in the world.

But first there was something I had to do. It was out there, calling. I could hear it in the rustle of the trees, in the songs of the birds. It called to me and only me.

It wasn't simple, learning how to blend in undetected and how to avoid the bullies but I worked out a way to do it at school, even if I couldn't at home.

The penny dropped one day when the doorbell sounded, echoing around the empty entrance hall of the house. I hadn't been used to being disturbed – no one ever visited us. Gingerly, I approached the door and opened it a crack, peering around to see who had disturbed my solitude. Standing in the early morning sunlight was a middle-aged man wearing a Royal Mail uniform.

'Delivery for'—the postman looked down at the parcel—'you?'

I hadn't been expecting anything but wanted to get rid of the intruder as soon as possible so accepted the package, mumbled a thank you and closed the door. Holding the brown paper parcel in my hands I turned it around a few times, inspecting it cautiously. It did indeed have my name on the label but I couldn't think who would send me anything or why.

Returning to the kitchen, where I had been reading happily before being disturbed, I sat back down on the rickety old chair and opened my post. As I did so an envelope fell to the floor. I inspected the writing, trying to identify the sender before putting it down on the table beside me.

Turning my attention back to the parcel I peeled the wrappings away carefully. Beneath the brown paper was another layer of colourful wrapping paper. It was sky blue crepe, which had been tied with a navy ribbon. It was a birthday present. I had almost forgotten that the day was approaching. Living in that house with Mummy, I felt the days all melted into one.

Putting the present down on my lap I picked up the card and removed it from its crisp white envelope. 'Many Happy Returns, Love Uncle Ross and Aunt Sharon'.

My uncle, Ross, lived somewhere up in Scotland with his wife Sharon. He was my mummy's brother and I had only met him once or twice in my life. He had never bothered to visit and I wondered why he was choosing to send me a birthday present now, for the first time ever.

But at fourteen years old my curiosity got the better of me and I ripped the wrapping off the gift, eager to learn what was inside. Inside was a green woollen jumper and a book. Holding the jumper up to get a better look at it, I decided it was the ugliest thing I had ever laid my eyes on and dropped it to the floor. The book was far more interesting. The faded red leather cover was old and worn. On the spine, embossed in gold text, were the words The Oxford Book of English Verse.

Holding the book up to my nose, I inhaled the smell of the musty paper before resting it in my lap and carefully turning the front cover.

My thoughts soon turned to the nondescript postman who appeared unexpectedly and who I opened my door to without hesitation. Such men exist and make their way through life without ever really being seen; I envied the way the postman remained more or less invisible.

Having adjusted my uniform in the mirror in the hall, so that my appearance was just right, the feeling returned once again and I closed my eyes for a moment, allowing myself to be swallowed by the weightlessness I carried inside.

That weekend, while I was walking along the lane, I was passed by a group of men on horses. If I'm honest, I'd never liked horses. They were large cumbersome creatures with staring, glossy eyes that made me feel awkward. They smelt like dung. Their muscles were unnatural. My admiration matched my distrust but I was excited as the hunt trotted past.

I ran along behind them for a while and noticed a dead fox hanging over the back of one of the horses. Its tail had been removed and only a bloody stump remained. It was barbaric. The smell of that blood is something I will never forget. It was my second introduction to death and it thrilled me more than I thought possible.

It is something I still dream about. That tail, which should have still been attached to the fox, soft at one end and the other wet and messy; the fleshy part of the stump looking like butchered meat.

I remember seeing a dead rabbit that Percy once caught. Its eyes were glazed over and had a cloudy film. But the rest of it was almost alive. Its fur still had sheen and the blood remained bright red – almost living.

That is my first and most vivid memory. It crawls through my body like an insect that marches with relentless precision. That is where it all started; on that wet autumn day in late September. The noise of the horses' hooves on the road, the gentlemen and ladies chatting gaily, the dogs barking and panting all swirled around in my head like an orchestra preparing to play.

There was one dog in particular that I watched with fascination. He was a large hound, white and tan, with dark eyes. Unlike the others that all pulled on their leads and sniffed each other's arses, he stood still and upright, his nose in the air searching for the scent he was waiting to follow. With his eyes half closed, his large black wet nostrils expanded sucking in the air. He was in his element. This was where he was meant to be. This is what he was born to do.

I know that hunting is controversial but there is something very beautiful about it. It is a primal desire to hunt. It's a desire that was inbuilt in those dogs, the same way a horse longs to gallop. Men have the desire to hunt, too. It is not something that is necessary anymore, society has put an end to that, but it remains, bubbling under the skin of people, looking for an escape.

On that day, watching the hunt, I realised I had it in me.

The Pica Explorer

Day five. Hour 21:30.

'Everyone stay calm.' Susie's voice is quivering. 'We need to get the torch.'

'It is in the drawer near the kettle,' Sam says.

'Okay. Please all stay where you are. I am going to try and feel my way.'

I hate the darkness. I always have but the darkness in the submarine is like no darkness I have ever experienced before. It is so thick it is almost alive. I start to think I can see shapes moving in it, the spirits of the dead people on board living in the blackness, walking among us. And then I think of the killer and wonder if they are in the room with me now.

'Hurry up, will you?' Frank's impatience is hugely irritating to me.

'She's doing her best,' I bite back as Susie clatters into something. 'Are you okay?' I reach out in the darkness hoping to make contact with someone but there is no one there.

'I'm fine.'

Someone is breathing very heavily close to me. Is it Frank? Is it Sam? The sound puts me on edge and I don't like it at all.

'Sam?' I speak into the darkness, not knowing in which direction to aim my words.

'I'm here.' His voice sounds further away than the breathing and I deduce that it must be Frank. Then the sound of a drawer opening grabs my attention.

'Got it,' Susie says, her words full of relief.

The next thing I see is a beam of bright light. It hits me directly in my eyes and I squint. Then the beam moves slowly around the room, looking for the others. It finds Sam before finally resting on Frank's face. The shadows cast on his features make his face look distorted and evil; like something from a horror film. His insane smile is repulsive.

'If the lights have gone, then the oxygen will probably be next,' Sam says from the darkness.

No one says anything. What is there to say?

Then from the distance we hear a banging sound. It travels through the darkness leaving behind visible vibrations in its wake.

'What's that?' Susie shines the torch light around the room, which darts about aimlessly as if it is a laser cutting through the black that surrounds us.

'It is coming from inside the sub,' Sam whispers loudly.

Frank's silence is unnerving.

The noise stops for a moment and then starts again. It is frantic and seems to be getting louder by the second.

'Luke!' Susie suddenly says. 'It's Luke.'

'What are we going to do?'

'Let's go.' The light searches for the door and I hear Susie crossing the room.

'Why? Are you going to let him out?' Sam sounds hoarse from fear.

'I don't know but we can't just leave him locked in there in the dark.'

'I think we can, actually.' Frank's low voice rises through the pitch-black darkness.

'Are you coming?' Susie turns and the light hits me again in the face.

'Yes. I'm not staying here.' I follow the lit pathway through the room when she lowers the torch.

'Fine,' Sam huffs. 'Come on then.'

'I'll be fine right here.' Frank remains standing in the darkness alone.

'Suit yourself.' Susie leads Sam and me in the direction that the clattering sound is coming from.

'Do you think he is safe left on his own?' I ask as we walk slowly, not able to see our feet.

'I don't care,' Sam snorts.

'We won't be long,' says Susie.

'I don't like this,' I admit. 'I don't want to die in the dark.'

I reach out and put my hands on Sam's back, which is just in front of me, and hold on to his clothing. He doesn't say anything but keeps on walking.

'This is crazy.' Suddenly Sam stops.

'What are you doing?' I lean in and ask. 'Susie, wait.' She spins around and the torch light whirls in the darkness.

'What is it?'

'I'm sick of this.' Sam reaches out his hand, searching until he finds mine. 'We can go and see if Luke is okay but then I'm going to go try fix the lights. There must be a way to get the power back on, if only for a while. I'm not ready to give up just yet.' Just then the noise from the room Luke is locked in comes to a halt.

'Do you know anything about electrics?' I ask with scepticism.

'Hopefully enough to come up with a temporary solution.' He squeezes my hand.

'Okay. But first let's just check on Luke. Deal?'

'Deal.' Sam nods his head and I admire his good looks for the first time in a few days. With everything that has happened it was easy to forget that I have been living side by side with a film star.

We walk faster now, grateful for the small amount of hope that Sam has offered us.

When we turn the corner Susie calls out to Luke.

'Luke. It's Susie.'

'Susie. You have to let me out.'

'Sorry, pal,' Sam replies, 'but that's not going to happen. We just came to see if you are okay.'

'I can't see anything. What's going on?'

'The lights have finally gone out,' I call back.

'Well, I can see that!' Luke shouts. 'Please, just let me out.' He starts banging on the door. 'I'm sorry. I know I frightened you all. I was just scared. But I'm fine now. Please.'

The three of us on the other side remain quiet.

'Come on, guys.' His voice starts to break.

'Maybe we should.' Susie points the torch to the bound door handle.

'Yes, yes, come on, Suz, just open the door.'

'He sounds much calmer.' Susie turns to us searching for agreement.

'I don't know,' I whimper, starting to feel dizzy.

'Not yet,' Sam says, taking control of the situation before turning to Susie and me. 'Ladies, let's go back to the living area. We can set up some candles and get you settled. I'll take the torch and go and see if there is anything I can do. If I manage to get the lights working then we will let him out.'

'And if you don't?'

'We will cross that bridge when we come to it. Right'—Sam leans over and takes the torch from Susie who relinquishes it without a fight—'we have a plan.'

'We'll come back for you.' Susie leans in and puts her hand on the door.

Sam starts to walk away and we follow, leaving Luke locked in the bunkroom screaming.

It doesn't take long for us to set up the living quarters with a few candles. The temperature has dropped noticeably and our breath clouds the air. Frank has been sitting in a corner the whole time not moving or saying a word. There is a strange expression on his face and his brow is furrowed.

Sam makes sure we both have a knife, some water and a blanket before he sets off.

'Keep an eye on him.' Sam turns in the doorway before disappearing. 'I won't be long.'

I huddle with Susie beneath the blanket, trying to get some warmth.

'Do you think this is it?' My teeth chatter and I struggle to get the words out.

'I don't know. I'm trying not to think about it,' she admits.

On the other side of the room, Frank seems oblivious to our conversation.

'We can't give up hope yet.' Susie puts her small head on my shoulder and I feel that she, too, is shaking from the cold.

The various candles dotted around don't offer much light but just enough for us to be able to see Frank's outline and the whites of his eyes.

'It's Frank who should be locked in that room, not Luke,' Susie whispers under her breath. She's right of course.

Rubbing my hands together furiously, I try to produce some warmth. 'I wish I was at home, with Olly.'

'Olly?' she inquires.

'Yes, my boyfriend.'

'You've never mentioned him before.'

'Haven't I?'

'No. How long have you been together?' She pulls the blanket up under her chin.

'A little less than a year. He's great.'

'Where did you meet?' It's very good of her to feign interest.

'In a bar. He makes great cocktails.'

'I love a good cocktail,' she agrees.

'Now I am never going to see him again. We had a fight before I left. I said some horrible things.' A lump forms in my throat.

'Hey, I'm sure he'll forgive you. At least you have someone. I don't really have any family or anyone.' She cuddles up to me even closer and I can smell her hair. It reminds me of something.

'I'm so cold.' I push the memory of Olly away. It is too painful.

'I know, me too.'

'And I'm tired. I'm so tired.' I rub my temples, knowing that something in my memory is stirring, trying to come out but it remains just out of reach.

'Come on.' Susie lies back and pulls me gently down. 'Close your eyes for a bit.'

'What about Frank?' I say looking over at the deranged man who remains sitting alone in the corner.

'I'll be awake.' She wipes a strand of hair away from my face. 'I couldn't sleep even if I wanted to.' Her words are spoken with sadness.

'Are you sure? Just for a little while. I'm feeling sick and my head is spinning.'

'Ssshh. Rest.' She puts her hand on my forehead to feel for a temperature, just like mothers do with their small children. 'You get some rest.'

Closing my eyes I hope to slip into sleep but colourful images dance behind my eyelids, twisting and turning in on themselves like a kaleidoscope while in the distance I think I can hear Luke calling out.

Turning onto my side, I hug myself beneath the covers and roll my body up into a foetal position in an attempt to get warm. But still my whole body trembles.

I lie there for a while, watching in awe as the swirling colours dance around in my mind and manage at last to find a brief moment of peace. Gradually I feel myself sinking into sleep and as I begin to allow the feeling to take hold I see a flash.

'Oh!' I feel Susie sit up next to me and I open my eyes.

I can see and for a moment it is surreal. The room is flooded with electric light and the brightness of it hurts my eyes.

'He did it!' Susie gasps in amazement. 'He bloody well did it!' She hugs me.

In the corner, I notice Frank has put his hands up over his eyes, much like a child playing hide and seek. He keeps them there and I motion to Susie to look up, watching as she slowly picks up the knife, concealing it under the blanket.

'Protection,' she mouths as if I didn't realise.

'Luke has stopped shouting.' My relief is tangible.

'Having the lights back on will make a big difference.' For the first time since we were plunged into darkness I feel my heartbeat returning to a semi-normal rate.

Moments later we hear running steps echoing down the corridor and shortly after that Sam appears in the doorway, sweaty and panting.

'Well done.' Susie rushes over to give him a hug but putting a hand up he stops her.

'The good news is that I managed to fix the lights.' He takes a long breath. 'For now.'

An impending sense of doom returns and I wait for him to continue.

'The bad news'—he hangs his head—'is that I found Anya.' Sam looks up and around at each of us in turn. 'She's dead.'

From the corner of my eye I see movement coming from Frank. He slowly lowers his hands from his eyes and speaks in a low voice.

'And then there were five.'

Susie

I've always been quiet and never one to rock the boat. I hate confrontation and always have ever since I was little.

Growing up I was a lonely child and I went through life trying to remain unseen. I suppose I was shy but I didn't mind my own company and it gave my imagination time to expand.

I loved animals as a young girl and would spend a lot of my time studying them and then doing drawings in my bedroom, which I hid beneath my bed because I was meant to be doing homework instead.

School wasn't much fun for me. The other children were mean and used to tease me, but I tried to keep my head down and keep out of their way. Sadly, the teachers never did anything about it, even though they knew what was going on.

When I was sixteen my mother died. My father hadn't been around and so I was sent to live with my uncle. He was better off than my mother and had a love of photography. I think he felt sorry for me, being an orphan, and he used to lend me his camera so I could go outside and take pictures of the birds and wildlife. That was when I developed my love of film. Life seemed so much more beautiful through a lens and for my eighteenth birthday he bought me a video camera. It was soon after that I left my uncle's home and went to London to carve out a career in film-making.

My uncle had some friends in London who showed me around and helped me to find my feet. The big city was a scary place, in comparison to the quiet countryside I'd grown up in, but I soon got used to it. The biggest hurdle was taking the Tube. I often got lost and ended up on the wrong side of the city.

Eventually I found a course in film-making. It wasn't one of the big, respectable film schools but it was an introduction and a step in the right direction.

Although my mother had not been wealthy she had at least owned the cottage we lived in and I was the sole beneficiary. That money helped me to pay for the course and my accommodation. Without meaning to, my mother had finally done something helpful.

After completing the course I managed to get little bits of work on small-fry productions and while on set, I realised that what I really wanted to do was become a producer. I'd always been quite organised and efficient so it seemed a good fit.

My first chance came when I was nearly thirty, in 2002, when I was given the job as production assistant with an advertising firm. I really learnt so much during my two years there and eventually found the courage to pursue working as a producer myself. Fortunately, the people at the company liked me and offered me a shot at stepping out of the shadows.

During my first ad, which was for a washing detergent, I was so nervous I couldn't eat a thing. I felt sick most of the time and my nerves were even worse when I had to show up on set.

The director, a nice guy who I think fancied me, was gentle and patient. For that I'll always be grateful. Everyone on set was great, as is usually the case. Of course there are exceptions but usually people on a set work out how to just get on. Nothing would ever get made if we spent our time bickering.

Gradually, I started to get a name for myself and after about eighteen months I was being offered lots of work.

I had a reputation for being easy to work with and I think that helped. No one wants to work with a tyrant, do they?

Having grown up with little money I was stunned by the amount I was making in advertising. I was able to buy myself expensive clothes and moved into a bright, airy apartment in Fulham.

Work became my sole focus and I had no time in my life for men. I'd always had trust issues with men and as an adult those did not subside. But I was content on my own. The flat was decorated just how I liked it and I didn't have anyone to answer to.

But things changed after the crash in 2009. Companies were spending less on adverting and the industry took a hit. Despite my reputation, and the various awards I'd received over the years, the work started to dry up and I ended up taking a job working on a really bad sitcom that was shown late at night when only teenagers and stoners were awake to watch it. The actors weren't great and the script was even worse, but it was work and it helped to pay my mortgage. Unlike other people in the industry I suppose I was lucky.

My luck changed yet again when I received a call from Frank Holden's PA out of the blue.

I'd heard the stories about Frank, as had many others, so I was curious when I was called to a meeting with the man, as well as cautious. His reputation preceded him and, as a reasonably attractive woman, I knew I needed to be wary.

Frank Holden was every bit as obnoxious as I'd heard he was but the thing that took me by surprise was his size. He was overweight and much taller than I had imagined. He was a man who commanded a room and I could see immediately why people were intimidated by him.

When I went into his ultra-modern office he remained seated in an expensive looking executive leather chair and sat with his hands folded and his chin resting on them. He wore a blue shirt that was tight around his belly. His small brown eyes looked me up and down before returning to the papers he had been reading before I was called in.

One his right sat a small woman dressed in black. She had cropped dark hair, and wore trendy black-rimmed glasses, which I suspected were not required for seeing, and bright red lipstick.

'Come in and have a seat, hon?' The American lady beamed.

I sat down on the opposite side of the huge glass desk feeling like I was a contestant on *The Apprentice*.

'I'm Monica Cherry, Mr Holden's PA. We're so glad you could join us today.'

I'd met many Americans who worked in film and was always surprised by the way they spoke. It was contrived but the familiarity of it was somehow comforting.

'Lovely to meet you.' I shifted in my seat feeling very small in the huge clinical office.

'Mr Holden is working on a new project and your name came to his attention.'

Frank would not look at me and sat back in his chair holding what I presumed was a script or film treatment.

'I've no real experience on feature films.' My throat felt dry and my voice was lost in the vast glass space.

'Not to worry. Mr Holden knows all about your experience. He has been impressed by what he has heard.'

I felt myself blushing. I'd never been comfortable with compliments, especially from strangers.

'Mr Holden needs a producer for his next movie. And he thinks you would be right for the job.' Her eyes fixed me through her fashionable glasses.

'I'm truly honoured.' I pulled the sleeves of my jumper down over my hands and fumbled with the fabric, feeling more like a little girl than a woman.

'Shooting will begin in four months.' Monica straightened some papers in front of her. 'Do you have any problem with water, hon?'

'Water?'

'Yes.' Frank leant forward and looked at me for the first time. 'You know, that wet stuff. The thing the sea is made out of. Water.'

'Oh, erm,' I stuttered, 'no, I like water.'

Frank sat back and roared with laughter and I felt my cheeks turn red.

'Good, because we are going to be immersed in it during filming.'

I looked at Monica, hoping she would shed some light on this bizarre conversation, but she had no intention of interfering with how Frank did things.

'I'm sorry,' I said finding my voice and some courage, 'but I don't quite understand.' The career woman in me decided enough was enough. I'd had too many years in my life when I'd been made to feel stupid. I wasn't about to return to those days.

'It's in a submarine, doll. That's where part of the film is set. You'll be on board for a few weeks, a couple of months at most. Think you can handle it?'

I took a moment to let it sink in. It was the strangest meeting I'd ever attended.

'I think I am up to it,' I lied, feeling extremely unsure.

'Don't look so frightened.' Frank smiled, showing all of his perfect Hollywood teeth. 'I don't bite.'

Monica suddenly looked extremely uncomfortable and adjusted her glasses. I wasn't sure how to respond.

'Look, doll, you don't need to worry. You're not my type. I like my girls curvy. Ironing boards just don't do it for me.'

I was speechless and Monica, who was clearly used to this kind of thing, did a brilliant job of deflecting the conversation.

'We are so thrilled to have you on board, Ms Sparrow. Someone will be in touch shortly with the schedule.' Monica got up out of her seat and came around the table. 'It has been a real pleasure meeting you, hon.' She put out her hand and I noticed her perfectly applied dark brown nail varnish. I also noticed that she wasn't 'curvy' and thought to myself she must be grateful for that.

Taken aback by the lack of information I'd been given and the bizarre discussion that had just taken place, I stood and shook her hand. For a second our eyes met and we shared a look. It was the type of moment that only two women can share. An unspoken understanding passed between us.

'Four months, doll, that's all you have.' Frank got up out of the chair, the leather squeaking as he did so. 'Think you can do it?'

'As soon as I have the information I need I will start work on the project.' I trembled slightly on my legs as I collected my bag from the floor beside me and allowed myself to be shown out by Monica who, despite her name, is nothing like a cherry.

Child

*A*fter Nick left Mummy stopped talking to me all together. When I came back from school or went downstairs in the morning she pretended I wasn't there. She stopped getting much food from the shops and instead ordered takeaways, or ready meals that were just for her. This went on for months.

One day, while I sat daydreaming in the lunch hall, I remembered Percy once muttering about the number of poisonous plants that we came into contact with on a daily basis and decided to investigate the matter myself.

It is amazing what you can learn from reading. Held within the pages of one book, that I found in the local library, was all the information about just how many dangerous plants grew wild in the English countryside. I took the book home and studied the contents, while a plan started to take form in my mind.

I learnt that hemlock, which is often found in riverbanks and ditches, can cause sickness if eaten and can kill by paralysing the lungs.

Foxgloves are also toxic. Despite the fact they grow in many gardens, they can cause diarrhoea, vomiting and even heart attacks if any part of the plant is eaten. But the most deadly plant in Britain is belladonna, often referred to as deadly nightshade. Although the roots are the most toxic, the whole plant can be fatal if an adult eats only a very small amount. The symptoms can be blurred vision, confusion, dilated pupils and convulsions. Finally, it attacks the nervous system and the ability to regulate breathing and heart rate. But the fact that amazed me most was that although it is extremely poisonous to humans and other domestic animals, rabbits and cattle seem to be able to eat the plant without suffering any harmful effects. Reading about

164

animals made me think about Robin. I closed the book and soon the tears came. As was often the case, I cried myself to sleep.

The next morning I woke unusually early. Sitting up in bed I listened to the chorus of the birds outside. It was a lovely sound and I felt my spirits lift until I was reminded that Robin was dead. Then I spotted the discarded book lying on the floor and realised what I needed to do.

I needed to poison Mummy.

After studying a lot more about the plant deadly nightshade, I learnt my best chance of finding it would be during the summer months in the woods.

The winter and spring went slowly and I became more and more withdrawn. School was awful and home felt like a prison.

By July, as the academic year came to an end, I could see a light at the end of a very black tunnel.

Mummy had removed anything of comfort from my bedroom in the winter and my bed no longer had a mattress. She said it had been soiled by my disgusting acts with Nick. She dragged it outside and set fire to it. The ground was scorched and the smell that lingered for some weeks after was rank.

When the long summer holidays arrived, I spent time in the woods searching for the special plant that I hoped would free me from my miserable life. It wasn't as easy to find as I'd hoped. I spent many hours scouring the woodland floor looking for the tall plant with its small flowers and dark berries. By August I was beginning to give up hope of ever finding it. Then, one day as I wandered through the woods a few miles from our house, I spotted it. A ray of light was filtering through the branches and leaves above, making the dark berries glisten.

I had read enough about the poisonous plant by then to know I needed to be careful, so I removed a pair of gloves from my pocket, put them on and held the plant carefully in my hand. It was as if it was talking to me, telling me to use it. The little berries looked a bit like blackcurrants. They were pretty. I picked a large handful and wrapped them in a tissue, which I put in my pocket, before skipping back through the woods in the direction of home.

That night, while Mummy slept, I crept downstairs and opened a kitchen cupboard. As I squashed the berries into a jar of jam I realised how fitting it was that nature would have its revenge on Mummy. Robin was still with me, willing me to do this and get justice.

It was ironic that one of the few things Mummy couldn't bring herself to stop buying was jam. She had it every morning on her toast. It was the one of the few things I had to eat. She always did have a sweet tooth.

Creeping back upstairs to bed I felt an excitement I'd never felt before. That night I didn't sleep. The anticipation was too much. Although I'd read a lot I didn't know what to expect. I had read that some people survived belladonna poisoning and hoped that it wouldn't be the case this time.

When I heard Mummy wake up and go downstairs I went and sat on the top step, listening intently for the sound of the toaster popping. When I heard the noise I almost squealed. I'd wished I could have sat opposite her and watched her stuff her face with her jam toast.

Fifteen minutes later she left for work. I spent all day patiently waiting for her to come home early suffering from illness but it didn't happen. When she strolled in at the normal time she appeared fine and my heart sank. But I knew it might be too soon to expect any reaction.

For the next three days that was my routine. I barely slept, and in the mornings sat on the stairs listening to her making her breakfast. Soon I began to wonder if the poison was working at all, but just as I was about to consider a different option, Mummy appeared home early one afternoon.

She came into the house and dropped her bag on the floor. I'd been sitting on an armchair in the living room reading when she returned.

'What are you looking at, worm?' Her voice sounded dry and sore.

I knew better than to answer back so I grabbed my book and legged it up the stairs to my bedroom. A few minutes later I heard her bedroom door close. Perhaps this was it.

Over the next few days she deteriorated slowly, complaining of blurred vision and feeling sick. Gradually her speech became slurred and she grew disorientated. As the end grew closer she was too weak to get out of bed.

I would stand in the doorway of her bedroom, looking at her with the same revulsion she had bestowed on me and it felt so good.

She was confused and hallucinating. Her pupils were dilated and occasionally she managed to beg me to bring her water, which I did. I wanted to prolong her pain.

Just over a week after she'd first ingested the berries she started to have fits.

***

Watching her die, I knew what I was supposed to feel. I was aware of how others would have reacted. They would have felt guilt and pity but I didn't. I couldn't. I felt relief and happiness.

I watched Mummy fade away with fascination. Her soft skin was stretched tight over her protruding collarbones and skinny shoulders. She hadn't eaten in days and had become fragile. At last she knew what it was like to be me.

I watched her as I would a mosquito under a microscope. The tiny hairs on her powerless body stood up, static as if with the excitement of being watched.

She became no more to me than a slab of meat and her dying gave off a sickly sweet smell of sweat and vomit.

Do you know what I'm talking about? Have you ever smelt it?

It's the odour that lingered beneath the scent of her cheap perfume and booze and cigarettes. It's a perfume like no other that speaks to the senses and draws you in. That alone is intoxicating. That alone would be excuse enough.

But I see more than that.

Below the smooth skin and bones I saw an entire network of life. The throbbing, bloody passages were a map. Beneath them the organs tried to pump and work to keep her body going but it was pointless. She was dying.

I would fantasise about seeing what was under her skin. To see it split, raw and bleeding just as it had been with Robin. I'd imagine a tool cutting through her flesh, just like when you split open a peach — the softness beneath my fingertips and the moisture beneath the velvet skin. Yes, I was right. Women are like peaches and I had waited until Mummy was ripe.

You think I'm stupid with my idioms. You'd prefer it if I came up with something entirely original. At least that is what you tell yourself. If I said I wanted to bury my face into the gashing wound of a dying woman, if that was the only thing that made me feel human, you'd turn away.

When I looked at her I saw an experiment, an opportunity to explore and learn something new. I saw more than just revenge.

Sadly, though, it stopped and she fell into a coma. My disappointment was bitter — I wanted her to suffer until the very end.

Rather than leave her like that I decided to have mercy. I wanted to show her that I was better than she was.

I took a knife from the kitchen, went upstairs to her bedroom and sliced open her throat.

I will never know if she felt a thing — but at last she was gone.

The Pica Explorer

Day five. Hour 22:00.

'A nya's dead?' I gasp. 'How? Who did it?'
'Let's just say it doesn't look like natural causes.' Sam's face is pale.
'Where is she?' Susie asks.
'She'—he gulps—'her head has been caved in.'
From the other side of the room Frank begins to chuckle. The laughter starts in his large belly and rises slowly until it settles in his throat by which time it sounds more like an animal is choking.
We do our best to continue our conversation, trying to ignore the violent and wild sound that is erupting from Frank.
'I can't stomach this smell and it's only going to get worse. Who is doing this to us? Why won't they stop?' My mouth fills with saliva and I have to swallow it down.
'I'm going to deal with it.' Sam smiles confidently 'Don't worry.'
'How?' Susie asks.
'I'm going to move them all into one room at the far end of the sub and try to seal the door.'
Imagining him having to carry those rotting, broken bodies made me feel even more queasy.
'You can't do it alone,' Susie says without offering to help.
'I can. What choice do I have?' The young selfish guy who first stepped onto The Pica Explorer has turned into a man right before my eyes. 'It's the right thing to do.' Sam turns his attention to Frank who remains cackling, still.

'How will you move them?' I ask, not really wanting to know the details but fascinated nonetheless.

'I haven't thought that far ahead. I'll work it out.' Sam shrugs. 'Will you both be okay if I leave you with him again?'

Susie and I look over at Frank, both being careful not to make eye contact with him.

'I don't understand what's happened. Why is he behaving so strangely? Why is everyone acting crazy?'

'It's the lack of oxygen,' Susie says. 'It makes people act oddly.'

'How do you know this stuff?' Sam asks.

'I used to read a lot as a child,' she admits. 'Look, we'll be fine. Just go.' Susie straightens up and nods decisively.

'You still have the knife?'

'Yes. Right here.' Susie pats her side.

Before leaving us again, Sam takes a moment to regain his composure before setting off to undertake his grim task.

'You don't have to do this.' I reach out and grab his hand. It is ice cold.

'Yes, I do.' He smiles briefly before disappearing again.

Susie and I remain standing by the doorway listening to his footsteps as they fade into the distance.

'He's very brave,' I say, trying to get the image of Anya's body out of my head. 'But what if it's actually him?'

'Yes.' Susie sounds distant and I wonder what she is thinking. 'Let's eat something. I fancy a jam sandwich. What about you?'

'The thought of food makes me feel quite sick if I'm honest.' I put my hand on my churning stomach. 'And I don't really like jam sandwiches. I'm not very hungry.'

'You should have something, even if it's small.' Susie sets about getting the bread and jam while I remain glued to the same spot, still cloaked in the blanket for warmth, looking down the corridor. I don't understand how she can eat at a time like this. Isn't she worried that a madman is on the loose?

I accept a slice of bread that is beginning to turn stale and tear off the crust, which I take small bites from.

Susie sits down at the table and starts tucking into her jam sandwich like a starving animal while I pick at my food, forcing myself to eat it.

From the other side of the room I see movement and swing my head to see that Frank is now standing up. He stretches and yawns like a big bear waking from hibernation. He scratches his stomach and then fixes me with a stare. I feel Susie tense and reach for the knife.

Frank shuffles over, moving awkwardly, and I wonder why. He stops just a foot away from where I am seated. He is a big man and his frame towers over me.

'Frank?' Susie shifts in her chair. His silence is troubling her too. He remains standing over me, looking down at me as if I am prey. 'Frank?' she asks again looking over at us.

It is at that point that he grabs me by the throat and pulls me up to face him. Drawing my face closer to his, he sticks out his fat tongue and proceeds to drag it down my cheek. As if I am watching this happen from a distance I hear Susie gasp.

His grip on my neck is tight enough to allow me to still breathe but too tight for me to cry out.

Then, with his other hand, he starts to fumble with the flies on his trousers. I try to turn to Susie to ask for help but I am frozen with fear. Seconds later she runs screaming out of the room leaving me alone with this monster.

'Pretty little thing, aren't you?' Frank runs his tongue over my mouth and I taste his foul breath as he slams me down onto the floor, lying down on top of me and pinning me to the ground with all his weight.

I close my eyes, unable to witness anymore, but cannot escape the noises of his grunting and the feel of his hands around the waistband of my trousers, trying to find a way in.

This is it, I think to myself. *This is the moment that I die.*

'If I'm going to die in this stinking place, I'm going to die fucking.' His words run through me like a shockwave. But then everything stops.

I can no longer hear the sound of his breathing or feel his heartbeat pressed against my chest. Suddenly everything is very still but he feels heavier than before. Something has changed.

When I open my eyes I see Susie and Sam standing over us. There is blood on Sam's hands and Frank's body has collapsed on top of mine making it difficult to breathe. A large knife is sticking out of his back.

Then the screaming begins, and it takes a moment before I realise that the sound is coming from me.

Child

*A*fter I killed her I sat down in a chair, where she used to do her make-up, and just looked at her for a while. She didn't look so scary anymore. She looked sort of sad.

The curtains had been closed and the room was quite dark. Outside I heard a bird cheeping and remembered Robin and the reason why I had done what I did. At last Mummy couldn't hurt anyone anymore.

I went over to the window and drew the curtains back. The sun was shining. I looked down into our overgrown garden and my eyes settled on the burnt mattress that lay at the end of the garden. The ground around it was black and scorched and it gave me an idea. That was where I would put Mummy: in the ground underneath the mattress. That is where I would bury her. It seemed fitting somehow. But I wasn't ready to let her go yet. I wanted her with me for a little while longer.

Looking down at my hands I saw that the blood had dried. It was reddish brown and cracked on my skin. I was reminded of the pottery I'd done at school.

Staring out of the window again, I felt sad remembering the day Mummy set fire to my mattress. I looked at her lying dead on her bed and had a thought. Then I went over to her and leant over. Her eyes were open and looking up at the ceiling but the light in them had disappeared.

I went around the bed unfolding all the corners of the sheets so that they were loose. Next, I wrapped them around Mummy and using all my strength pulled her off the bed and onto the floor. She hit the carpet with a thud. Her mattress was stained with blood so I flipped it over. It was surprisingly heavy. The other side was clean. This would be my *new bed and my bedroom from now on. Mummy could just stay there on the floor for a while.*

I got onto the bed and curled up, the warm sun flooded through the window onto my back, and I closed my eyes. It was the best sleep I'd ever had.

When I woke up, a few hours later, I got off the bed, stepped over Mummy and went downstairs. I was now the boss of the house and I wanted to make it my own. I went through the kitchen reorganising everything in a daze. It felt so surreal to be able to move around the place without the fear of being yelled at or beaten.

I made sure to take the jam out of the cupboard and put it in the bin at the front of the house then I made a start on the living room.

Mummy used to be mean about the fact that I like to read and I took pleasure in binning all of her DVDs, even though I liked films, to make space for the books I planned to read and collect. I moved the TV upstairs into my new bedroom so that I could watch it in bed, which is something Mummy would never have let me do. Her body remained on the floor as I set it up and it felt like she was watching me. But I liked the feeling she might be watching and couldn't do anything about it. It made me feel powerful.

The next thing I did was to write a letter to Mummy's work, from Mummy, telling them that she quit and had found another job. I would post it the next day.

I spent the next two days doing exactly as I pleased and it was bliss. I ate what I wanted and went to bed when I felt like it. Everything was great but it was soon spoiled, once again, by Mummy.

The smell was vile but I could just about cope with that, because I kept the bedroom window wide open. But when the maggots and the flies settled in I knew it was time to move her. They came and started living off Mummy. It was disgusting.

I went into the shed in the garden and found a spade. After dragging the burnt remains of my old mattress out of the way I started to dig a hole in the large charred part of the ground. It was hot and tiring work. I dug for hours until I was sure the grave was deep enough before clambering out of the hole, sweaty and covered in earth. It made sense to wait until it was dark to drag her down the stairs and into her final resting place. I would have to fill it in under the cover of night.

When my work was done I got myself a picnic and went and sat in the garden. The weather was good and I was pleased to be away from the rotting smell and the flies that now buzzed around the house. After lunch I settled down with a book I'd borrowed from the library and enjoyed the sunshine.

When darkness fell I was ready to move Mummy – but I knew it wouldn't be easy.

I had to tug her along the landing wrapped in the blood-stained sheet, which actually made it easier. It also meant I didn't have to touch her decaying body. The flies left her in a black cloud and I noticed that her corpse had gone stiff as I started to move it. When I'd managed to position the body at the top of the stairs, I had to give it a hard shove to get it to fall down. She fell awkwardly and I am pretty sure some of her bones broke as she tumbled.

I stood at the top of the stairs for a moment looking down at Mummy's crumpled corpse. An arm was sticking out from beneath the sheet and the skin looked all grey and mottled.

By the time I got her to the edge of the grave I was exhausted. As I bent down so that I could roll her in, I felt a twinge of sadness. This would be the last time I would ever see her. I had enjoyed spending time with her over the last few days. It was nice being with her when she wasn't angry. But I knew the moment couldn't last and I said goodbye as I pushed her into the deep dark hole before piling the earth on top of her and patting it down, then dragging the mattress back over the gravesite.

That week I concentrated on applying for part-time jobs. Although I hated school I knew I had to keep attending otherwise it would arouse suspicion. Luckily, I knew the pin code for Mummy's credit card so I was able to live off her savings. She'd inherited a bit from her parents and I was surprised and delighted to discover she had over fifteen thousand pounds in her account. I would be able to survive off that for some time as long as I kept it topped up with some money

Betsy Reavley

from a part-time job. Mummy didn't have a mortgage, either, so all I had to do was have enough for the bills and food.

For once everything was falling into place without any difficulty and I planned to make as much as I could out of my new life.

The Pica Explorer

I must have fainted because when I come round, Frank's dead body is no longer lying on top of me and I am able to sit up freely. His large torso has been rolled over onto his side and his small piggy eyes are staring at me, glazed with shock.

Scrabbling on my bum, away from the dead man, I end up backing into a chair and hitting my elbow on a metal leg.

Susie is standing glued to the spot, her hand over her open mouth, looking down at Frank in horror, while Sam remains motionless. All of the colour has drained from his face.

'What did you do?' Susie stammers.

I look down at my hands, seeing they have blood on them and watch as they begin to shake uncontrollably.

'I... I...' Sam swallows hard. 'I actually did it.'

Susie, to my surprise, takes a step towards Frank and stands over the body for a minute before bending down and taking hold of his wrist to check his pulse.

'He's gone,' she tells us, closing her eyes and shaking her head.

'You saved me.' My eyes fill with tears and I look up at Sam who is looking down at his own hands in awe.

'I did it,' Sam says again, sounding proud rather than ashamed.

'We know you were only trying to save Zara.' Susie gets up. 'It was an accident. We know that.'

'I did it,' he says again and a smile creeps across his face. 'After all this time...' His words fade away.

Susie and I share a look of concern. Where is the remorse?

'You're in shock. It's okay, just sit down for a moment.' Susie tries to guide Sam over to a seat but he won't budge.

'You don't understand!' He lets a little laugh escape. 'You don't get it.'

'Sam, you're not making any sense.' Susie puts her arm on his shoulder and he flinches.

'My mother.' Sam stops and swallows hard. 'Frank killed her.'

Now I know that Sam has lost the plot and I wish I was anywhere else but here.

'He raped her when she went to America. She never recovered.'

I try to tell myself that this is all insane but, given what just happened to me, I decide to hear Sam's story.

'I was a child when she went to New York. She was offered a role on Broadway and she was gone for a few months. When she got back she was a different woman. Sad all the time, tearful and had lost the light in her eyes. None of us understood what was wrong. My brother and I thought that maybe she was sad to be back with us and was missing the stage, but then one night I heard her tell my father what had happened. Frank had come backstage, promising her he wanted to talk about a big role he had coming up that she would be perfect for. Then he raped her. She never told anyone – she was so ashamed. It broke her.'

I can't help looking at the body of the man Sam is talking about and all I feel is relief.

'He was a vicious piece of work,' Sam continues, trying to justify his actions to himself. 'My mother killed herself because of him. Our family was never the same again. My father fell apart and I have never forgiven this pig for what he did to her. He might as well have murdered her himself.' Sam leans over and spits on Frank's body. 'Good riddance to bad rubbish.' He wipes his mouth with the back of his hand.

Susie slowly moves over towards me and encourages me to get up off the floor while Sam's tirade continues.

'I found her body. I will never forget the moment I came home and found her dead. I was a boy, a young kid, and it destroyed my life. At her funeral, standing by her grave, I promised my mother I'd have my revenge.' He starts circling Frank's body like a vulture and once again I don't feel safe.

'I became an actor because I was determined to find a way to make Frank pay for what he did to her.'

My head pounds and the room begins to feel very small, as if it is closing in around me.

'I didn't know it would end like this. I wanted him to hurt but I didn't know the sub would sink. I could never have foreseen that. None of us could. But watching him lose control, watching him suffer has made this all worth it.' Sam stops and lifts his right foot, before resting it above Frank's face for a moment. 'The monster is dead!' he yells and brings his shoe down onto Frank's cheek slowly and deliberately. 'Eat shit!' He spits on Frank again.

'You've suffered a terrible thing,' Susie agrees, taking small steps backwards towards the exit pulling me with her, 'but it's over now.'

'No.' Sam shakes his head sadly. 'Not quite.' Susie and I freeze, not wanting to antagonise Sam in any way.

'Yes, it is. He's dead,' she speaks softly.

'We are all dying,' Sam says wistfully as he struggles to remove the large knife that is sticking out of Frank's broad back. 'It's over.' He looks down at the blood-covered blade, which is now missing its tip. 'You need to leave.' Sam turns to us with a sombre expression. 'Now.'

'What are you going to do?' My words come out in a squeak.

'It's time for me to join my mother.' Sam lifts the knife to his own throat and closes his eyes.

'You don't have to do this.' Susie lunges forward with her arms outstretched. 'Please.'

'Go.' He opens his eyes and we know he is serious.

'Come on'—I pull Susie's arm—'we need to leave.' As we fall back into the corridor I hear a gurgling sound and spluttering coming from the living area and slam the door shut with my foot.

'It's just us now,' Susie says as a single tear rolls down her pale cheek.

'And Luke,' I add looking over at the locked door that contains the only living male on board.

Child

*A*t sixteen I left the small village I'd spent my life in and moved to a city to attend sixth form. I'd considered going straight to London but the thought of the big city was too daunting. I'd once been on a day trip to the city with the school, to visit the historic centre. It seemed like a nice place and so I decided to make it my new home.

Pretending to be Mummy, I arranged for an ad to go into the local paper and rented out the house. I couldn't sell it without raising suspicion so renting it out was my best option. Besides, it would give me a monthly income that would allow me to study properly.

During the summer term, after my sixteenth birthday, I paid the city a visit one weekend and arranged a tour of a sixth form college, which was one of the most prestigious in our area. It was so much more than I could have expected, so different to the over-subscribed, run-down school I'd attended. I knew, as I walked around the building, that it was where I wanted to be. All I had to do was make sure that my exam results were suitable.

That same day I took a big gamble and found a room to lodge in. If I wanted to get into that sixth form then I needed a local address.

On a road, very close to the college and the station, stood a number of grand Victorian houses. In one of them lived an old lady called Mrs Sturdy. She was a widow in her eighties who rented out the numerous spare bedrooms in her large home and had done so for years.

She showed me around the house, explaining I could use the kitchen and that I had shared bathroom facilities before showing me the bedroom, which was at the top of the house in the attic. It wasn't the largest room but it had a bed, wardrobe, chest of drawers and desk.

The monthly rent included all bills and more importantly it was an easy walk to the college.

I gave Mrs Sturdy a cash deposit and said I intended to move in during late July. She asked me why my parents hadn't come with me to see the house and I had explained they were busy working. The lie rolled off my tongue with ease.

Mrs Sturdy was a strange little old woman, whose back was very bent. She smelt of rosewater and urine. It was an odd combination. From our first meeting it was clear to me that she would not interfere with my life as long as I paid my rent on time, which suited me down to the ground.

I was introduced to the other lodgers in the house. One was a Chinese man by the name of Wang Li. He didn't speak to me very much and spent a lot of time in the kitchen cooking. He was harmless enough. In the room opposite me lived a fat girl called Lucy. She had a permanent scowl on her face and I often saw her sitting on her bed eating biscuits while studying. Whenever she saw me looking she would slam the door. I didn't like her. She used to look at me like I was a pervert.

The other residents of 49 Barnabus Road included a man in his forties who was a computer technician. He was only there from Monday to Friday and had a family in Wellingborough, near Northampton, who he returned to every weekend. There was a Polish couple in one of the rooms, who I often heard arguing in Polish. And lastly there was a Cambodian nurse. She was a small and gentle woman who was a bit lost on her own in the city. She worked in a large teaching hospital so that she could send money home to her family in Siem Reap. Her English was lousy but she tried her best and would often offer me her leftovers. She always cooked far too much.

Returning to the cottage in the countryside, I set about making it fit to be rented out. That meant moving the mattress, which had lain discarded in the garden for a few years. The only way to get rid of it for good was to douse it in petrol and set it alight. I felt nothing as I watched the angry flames devour the fabric and when the ground was no longer hot I raked it, making it ready for grass seed, which I planted a few days later.

It didn't take very long for me to get the garden looking respectable. No one would ever know the secret it concealed.

***

After learning that I'd achieved the right grades to go to Hills Road, I packed up all of Mummy's belongings and took them to a charity shop. After that I was ready to leave the cottage for the last time.

It had been easy arranging for an estate agency to take on the house. They didn't need anything more from me than Mummy's signature, which I'd become an expert at faking.

I delivered the keys to them in an envelope and then got a bus to the train station. I knew it would be the last time I'd ever set foot in that village or that house.

By September I was raring to start college. I'd decided that photography would be my main focus alongside English.

During the four weeks I'd spent living at 49 Barnabus Road I'd also worked on changing my appearance. I was sick of being the child everyone bullied. I got new clothes, like those I'd seen the other cool kids wear, started to listen to the music I knew they liked and got my hair cut. I put posters up on my wall of the films that I'd heard classmates talk about and made sure I was unrecognisable as the kid who'd lived in Suffolk.

On that first day I walked into my new classroom at Hills Road with my head held high. All the shit from my past felt like a distant memory and I now had an opportunity to rewrite history and make something of myself. At last I was really free from Mummy.

The first few months were great. I enjoyed the course, the teachers were easy-going but engaging and I made a lot of friends, but as Christmas approached I started to have problems. I'd have moments where I'd black out and then start to panic.

One of the nicer tutors took me aside and suggested I met with the college counsellor. I didn't like the idea of it at first. I had more pride than that but as the problem escalated and began to interfere with my work, I realised I didn't have a choice.

For a few weeks I had regular appointments with Ed Potter. He was nice enough and eager to help. He listened to me describe what *was happening to me and how I felt, without interrupting. I never mentioned Mummy or my family. I pretended that Cynthia Sturdy was my grandmother who I lived with. No one ever questioned any of it.*

After a few sessions with Ed he sat me down and said he was concerned I was suffering from post-traumatic stress disorder, otherwise known as PTSD. He asked me if there had been an event in my life that could have sparked this.

Unable to reveal the truth, I explained that my parents had died in a car crash when I was small and that was why I lived with my grandmother. He told me that it was possible I'd suppressed feelings from that time and that would explain why I was suffering with the symptoms. Ed advised that I made an appointment to see my GP to discuss this further. I promised I would as I left his office.

I had no intention of visiting a doctor or talking to Ed about any of this again. Instead I did my own research on the disorder. For the last few years I'd been used to dealing with things on my own. I didn't need a doctor or a shrink getting involved and digging about in my life. I couldn't risk jeopardising everything I had worked so hard to achieve. It was too late for Mummy but I still had a chance to have a good and happy life.

Like I'd always done, I turned to books and research to learn as much as I could. It quickly became clear that Ed had come up with the right diagnosis. My symptoms were a classic case of PTSD and I could feel the pressure building. The insomnia I'd been suffering, the nightmares and the blackouts all suggested I was suffering from the disorder. But I refused to seek medical help. There would be too many questions. I had to find a way to cope with this myself and I set about working out a lifestyle plan that would keep it at bay.

I had come so far. I wasn't ready to give in yet. The same way I had dealt with Mummy by myself, I would deal with this alone.

The Pica Explorer

Day six. Hour 00:20.

'I'm tired, Susie. I'm so tired.' I lean my head against the cold wall and feel the life seeping out of my bones. 'I can't fight anymore. It's pointless.'

'What are we going to do?' She cuddles up to me and nuzzles her head into mine.

'Let's go and lie down, just for a little while.'

'It's the lack of oxygen,' Susie says, sniffing back tears.

'I don't care anymore. Let's just go to sleep for a bit.'

'Okay.' She wipes her eyes and we make our way to the only comfortable room left where we can lie in peace, away from the bodies that litter the submarine.

'It's so cold.' Susie shivers, reaching for a large coat that hangs on a hook on the back of the door. 'Here, we can use this as a cover.'

We go over to the bottom bunk and pull as many layers as we can over ourselves for heat before lying down next to one another. Our breath clouds the air and breathing is beginning to feel difficult.

'Just a short sleep. That's all,' I say, closing my eyes, no longer able to fight the fatigue.

'Yes, rest.' Susie yawns and I feel her tense body relax a little.

Sleep comes within seconds and the horror of our prison melts away into oblivion.

I wake some time later in a cold sweat. Nightmares have plagued my sleep and I don't feel rested at all. Susie tosses and turns next to me, trapped inside her own troubled mind. I ease away from her, not wanting to wake her despite the pained look on her sleeping face.

Standing up, still feeling drowsy, I listen to the sound of the submarine all around me. The creak of the metal, the sound of my shallow breathing, the little sighs that come from Susie. I know I am dying. We both are and there is nothing I can do to change that.

I imagine people on the surface, hundreds of metres above, trying to solve the mystery of our disappearance. It's hard to believe that with all the technology man has invented, they cannot find us. But then I think about the size and depth of the ocean and I realise it isn't a surprise. It must be like looking for a needle in a haystack, or a drop in the ocean...

We are truly lost and this is where we will rest.

All I wanted to do was make films. I wanted to have a happy, easy life. One day I'd planned to have a family of my own, a house in the country perhaps. This was not how it was meant to end.

I slump to the floor and let the hopelessness of the situation take over. My body shakes, my stomach twists into knots and the room spins as if I am on a merry-go-round. Maybe this is all just a bad dream. Perhaps I am imagining it all. Maybe none of them exist and I'm not on the submarine at all, just trapped inside a very long and realistic nightmare that refuses to let me go.

Just when I think I am going to pass out, or die, something brings me back into reality. A sound. Something far away that is growing closer with each thud. I hear it like a beating drum rattling around my skull, echoing in my bones. The sound of my breathing fades into the background and all I can hear is that sound.

With a start Susie sits bolt upright, banging her head and cussing as she does so. 'What is that noise?' she asks, rubbing her head.

'You can hear it too?' I feel instant relief. I am not going mad.

'Yes.' She cranes her head to try and work out what direction it is coming from. Then the penny drops.

'Luke.' It hits me like a eureka moment. 'It must be Luke.'

'What do we do?' Susie pulls her knees up to her chin and hugs herself.

The two of us remain listening for some time as the sound gradually fades as if he is losing the energy to carry on. Then it stops.

Susie and I sit looking at each other with bated breath, waiting for the banging to start again.

'Maybe he's dead,' I mouth, not wanting to shatter the welcome silence.

'Maybe he's not.' Susie's wide eyes are fixed on the door.

'Let's lock ourselves in.' I get to my feet, feeling shaky. 'Come on, help me secure the door. It sounds like he might have got out.'

'There's nothing in here. No food, no water.' She begins to panic.

'Okay, okay.' I bend over and put my head between my legs, trying to suck in air to stop myself from passing out. 'Let's get some supplies.'

'I'll go.' Susie pulls back the layers she had been sleeping under and bolts towards the door. 'Stay here. If I'm not back in a few minutes, then find somewhere to hide.'

'You can't.' I reach out as she disappears.

Those few moments alone in the room seem to last a lifetime. Luke is no longer making any sound and I can't hear or see any sign of Susie. I don't want to die in this room alone. Susie has been the only thing that has kept me going. I need her to come back and for the first time in my life I pray. I get on my knees and ask God to save me, to save us. My hands are pressed tightly together and I repeat the words over and over again.

Like a miracle, when my eyes open, I see Susie standing there. Her arms are full of supplies and I scrabble to stand and hug her tightly.

'Thank you,' I cry into her hair. 'Thank you.'

She puts what she has collected on a table and grabs hold of a bottle of whisky.

'Let's go out with a bang.' She smiles through her tears.

'You made it. You've saved us.'

Susie looks at me strangely. 'We need to lock that door. The door to the room Luke was in is now open. He's out there somewhere.' She grabs a chair and props it up against the handle. 'I got all the food I could see. There isn't much.' She pants, tired from the energy it has taken to get the food and lock us in. 'So this is it.'

'Okay.' I nod, looking at the meagre amount that is left to sustain us. 'I guess it's just you and me now.'

Child

*E*verything had been good at first. The relationship grew quickly from nothing. Our attraction was instant.

We met in a bar and got chatting, and the next thing I knew we were in bed. For weeks we spent as much time in each other's company as possible. We'd both been in London for a while and were both starting out on our new career paths. We were like two sides of the same coin. One of us was led by their head, the other by their heart. There was a balance that worked and was harmonious. I'd found my soulmate and the person I was meant to be with.

It took some time before we decided to live together. Neither of us wanted to rush into that and risk spoiling what we had.

In the evenings we would meet and have long dinners, chatting, laughing, sharing our hopes and fears. It became difficult to tell where one started and the other one ended but that was all part of the magic.

The excitement in the early days was tangible. Meeting someone who I connected with so closely left me floating on a cloud. I never knew love like that could exist. I'd never been loved in my life. I'd only ever felt it once and that had been for a little bird.

I felt complete at last, as if what had been taken away from me, when Robin was killed, had now been replaced with something even better.

I knew then that my life would be good and everything bad that had happened was now firmly in the past where it belonged.

As is natural at the start of any relationship, questions were asked about my upbringing, where I'd come from and who my family were but I managed to deal with these with ease. I never lied, I just avoided telling the truth. It was my job to protect this new love from the vile truth of my childhood. And I was no longer that person so it wouldn't *have done any good to share it. I had transformed into something new. Like a butterfly, I'd shed the ugly cocoon that had kept me trapped as a child and now I was a proud, confident and successful adult. That was the person I wanted my lover to see.*

When we decided to take the plunge and move in together it felt like the natural thing to do. All of our spare time was spent together anyway and we missed each other terribly when we were apart.

I will never forget that thrilling moment when we collected our keys. I was amazed that something so small, which was made of metal, could make me feel so much happiness.

We lived together for months without any problems. It didn't take long for us to discuss marriage and children. We wanted a future together and it felt, for the first time, that I had landed in the right place. I was with the person I was meant to be with; someone kind and good. Someone who never pushed me or asked me to be anything other than what I was.

Our flat wasn't the nicest in London but it was our little haven. It was a place I felt safe and a home where we grew closer and made plans.

We put our own stamp on it, decorating it in a way we both liked despite having different tastes. But that is the thing about love, it is about compromise – it is about understanding each other's differences and making room for them. Not once did either of us try to change the other.

The other special thing about our relationship was how supportive we were of each other's careers. Our jobs were very different but we encouraged each other to strive for more.

When I came home and revealed that I'd been offered a job working with Frank Holden I was given the warmest hug and congratulations. I was so thrilled with the opportunity and what it meant that I began to cry.

It was in that moment that everything changed and my past came flooding into the future.

'Don't cry. This is a good thing. Be happy.' We kissed and I felt wonderful. 'You just need one of my special hugs...'

I backed away full of terror, tripping over a rug as I put distance between our bodies. Before I had a moment more to think, I picked up a large vase and threw it across the room at my love.

It hit the wall and smashed into a thousand pieces.

'What's wrong, darling?' My love couldn't understand what was wrong.

'Special hug?' My lower lip trembled, which sent a wave of shock through my body.

'Yes, all you need is a special hug.'

On a table near the sofa I saw a pair of scissors and grabbed them. Before I knew what was happening I was plunging them into the chest of my lover over and over again.

'How could you!' I cried when the body stopped moving. 'I thought you were the one. It was a trick. You were just pretending when you were him all along.'

Crying, covered in blood and exhausted, I finally fell asleep next to the corpse. When I woke and saw what I'd done I knew I would never escape from Mummy or what had happened to me. With those few words my life had done a somersault and I was thrown back into the past again.

I got up and removed a blue blanket from the sofa and covered my love with it.

'Shhh, darling. Sleep.' I wiped the blood off on my hands and onto my trousers. 'I am going to have a shower now. Look at the state of me.' Stepping over the body I turned back to have another look. 'I'll see you later. Don't go anywhere.'

The Pica Explorer

Day six. Hour 06:00.

We sit and drink the whisky like our lives depend on it. I've never been much of a drinker. I don't like the blackouts or feeling like I am losing control but here, with Susie, in this godforsaken situation, I embrace the fog that alcohol has to offer.

She glugs from the bottle like a pro. Each sip I take burns my throat and makes me gag.

I watch, as gradually her shoulders relax and her speech becomes slurred. The whisky is working its magic.

'What's the point?' she mumbles. 'We might as well drink ourselves to death, eh?' She takes another large mouthful of the honey liquor; a small drop escapes her mouth and runs down her chin before she hiccups. 'So, Zara-Zoo, what are you going to miss about your life?' She lies back onto a pile of clothes and blankets, and closes her eyes. 'Tell me.'

I try to think for a moment. *What will I miss?*

'Come on,' she encourages, swinging the bottle in her hand, 'there must be something. What about your chap, what was his name, erm, Oscar?'

'Olly.' The whisky is swishing in my stomach like the waves in the ocean that is holding us captive. 'His name was Olly.'

'Was?' She sits up and hiccups again.

'I won't see him again.'

'That's true.' A sad expression settles on her face and she lies down again.

'Just get some sleep.' I get up and go over to her, pulling a coat from underneath her and covering her with it. 'You're drunk.'

'Maybe if you got drunk you'd feel better,' she slurs, fighting the urge to pass out.

'I don't like it when people get drunk,' I sigh. 'It reminds me of my mummy.'

Seconds later Susie has dropped the bottle and is fast asleep.

I pull a chair over to look at her. She is small and fragile, just like Robin was.

'I can't believe I found you again, little bird.' My hand reaches out and brushes the hair from her face.

Susie moves in her sleep, completely unaware of the new situation she is in.

'I knew we'd be together again one day,' I whisper, making sure that the strips of fabric I'm using to tie Susie to her chair are secure. I sit back to admire my friend as her head lolls about in a drunken daze.

Then I open a packet of digestive biscuits and munch on one while I wait for Susie to come round. It tastes good although my throat is raw from the whisky.

Gradually Susie starts to wake up and I'm filled with excitement.

'Come on, little bird,' I encourage, 'wakey, wakey.'

When she opens her eyes, it takes her a moment to realise she is restrained. 'What the...' Susie wriggles in her chair. 'Zara?' Confusion clouds her face.

'There you are! I've been waiting for you.'

She looks down at her bound feet and tries to tug at the fabric that keeps her hands tied behind her back.

'What are you doing?' Susie stutters.

'I promise'—I inch closer—'this is for your own sake. It's to keep you safe. I don't want you flying away again now, do I.'

She shivers, probably as a result of the cold, and I fetch her a coat, which I drape across her shoulders.

'I brought you some food.' Removing another biscuit from the pack I crumble it up and shake some into the palm of my hand.

Susie looks at me with horror. 'Just a little bit now. We don't want you getting fat.'

'Please,' she moans.

'I'm going to take care of you. I won't let you go again, little bird.' I brush the biscuit crumbs onto the floor.

'My name is Susie. Susie Sparrow. Not little bird. Zara, what are you doing?'

'You can't fool me.' I chuckle. 'I knew it was you from the moment we met. I could sense you'd come back to me.'

'Please, Zara, just let me go. I'll be good. I promise I'll be good.'

Cocking my head, I look at her for a moment wondering if she really believes that I might free her.

Her thin lips are a bluish shade of purple and her teeth are chattering. Her body cowers against the chair and I notice how her collarbone sticks out more than it did when I first saw her.

'You should eat. It's important. I want you to survive. That's why I did all of this. So we could be together at the end.'

'I don't understand,' Susie wails, trying to free herself and rocking backwards and forwards as the chair threatens to tip over.

'Now, now. You don't want to make me cross.' I stand up and put my hands on my hips.

'What do you want from me? Please, Zara, I don't understand.' Susie stops rocking on the chair and looks up at me, frightened, like a little bird.

'You need to eat. I've done everything I can to make sure you and I survive. I got rid of all of those bad people just for you. The least you can do is show me some gratitude.' I feel anger rising in me now and I want to control it. I don't like being cross with Robin.

She sits motionless, staring up at me; her mouth partly open, and I take the opportunity to put a biscuit in her mouth. It makes her cough and splutter. Crumbs fall down her front and litter the ground.

'Ungrateful.' I slap her face hard. 'You need to learn some manners.'

'I'm sorry,' Susie apologises. 'I'll eat it. I will. Please give me another chance.'

Still cross, but not wanting to hurt Robin again, I break off another piece of digestive and offer it to her. She takes a large mouthful.

'Greedy little bird,' I mutter as I back away and watch her eat from a distance. 'Greedy, greedy, little bird.'

She swallows the mouthful of dry biscuit with difficulty, so I offer her some water, which she gulps down gratefully.

'Don't worry, little bird.' I cup her head in my hands and bend down on my heels. 'You look scared.'

Sitting down on the dusty floor I grow accustomed to the low light in the room. She refuses to meet my eye.

'Sing for me.'

She lifts her head, showing me her sad eyes and gaunt face.

'Please?'

She shakes her head.

'But that is why I brought you here. I want you to sing.'

'I can't do it…' Her voice is broken and a tear rolls down her white cheek. 'I won't.'

Letting out a long sigh I get up off the floor and dust myself off.

'If you will not sing then I no longer have any use for you,' I say, moving over to the table where a knife is laid out.

'Wait, please.' The words trip out of her mouth. 'Can you just explain it all to me? I need to understand. You owe me that much. I'm your little bird. You owe me that much.'

I turn my back to the table and I have to tear my eyes away from the glinting blade.

'Very well. I will tell you everything but I don't think you are going to like it.'

She sits there while I tell her all about Mummy and Robin. Her face doesn't flinch but her eyes say everything.

'And then Olly.' I pause. 'I thought he was the one, I really did. Why did he have to say that? Why did he have to use those words? It was all going so well. I'd got my life on track.' It is my turn to feel pain now.

'It's not your fault,' Susie says gently. 'Your mother was abusive. She didn't give you a choice. You were a child.'

'Mummy couldn't help herself,' I agree.

'But you have a choice now. You don't have to be like her—'

'What?' I interrupt.

'I mean'—she hesitates—'you can be kind. You can be gentle and forgiving.'

'I am nothing like her,' I spit. 'She made me hurt her. Just like Olly and the others. Don't you understand? I only got rid of them so that we could be together. The oxygen, you said it yourself, there isn't enough for everyone. They were bad people: Anya, Ray. All bad people. They didn't deserve the air they breathed. But you do, little bird, and so do I. That's why I did it. For us.'

Susie hangs her head and lets out a long pained sigh.

'Do you want me to sing?' she asks, her head still resting on her chest.

'More than anything.' I sink to my knees.

'Then you need to untie me. What good is a bird that doesn't have its wings?'

I pause for a moment and think about what she is saying. It does make sense but I'm frightened. 'I don't want you to go away again, Robin. I've been so lonely.' I start to cry.

'It's okay. Really, Zara, I'm here. I will sing if you just let me go. A bird needs its freedom. It's not like I can really leave anyway. Where would I go? We are trapped here. There is no way out.' Her soft voice calms me. 'I was your little bird then and I want to be the same little bird now but you have to give me my freedom.'

'And you promise you won't try and fly away?'

'I have nowhere else to go.' She smiles sadly.

'Everything we need is here.' I get to my feet and approach her cautiously.

'Yes, it is,' she encourages.

'I'm so happy to have you back. You don't know how much I've missed you.' My hands are shaking with emotion and I struggle to loosen the ties around her wrist.

Once freed she rubs her wrists and smiles at me. 'Thank you,' she says in a shaky voice. 'Now my feet. Can you untie my feet?'

'What are you going to sing?' I ask as I begin to fiddle with the restraints.

'What would you like to hear?'

'Oh, that's a tough one. I have so many favourite songs.' I find myself thinking back to my childhood and imagining the songs Mummy might have sung to me had things been different. 'Do you know 'Hush, Little Baby'?'

'Yes.' She swallows hard. 'I know it well.'

Just as I free her feet she kicks out violently, knocking me back.

'You lied!' I cry with hurt.

'Luke!' she screams. 'Luke, help me!'

Then Susie charges at me with all her might and we tumble to the floor as she pulls at my hair. But I am stronger than her and it doesn't take long before I have gained control by getting her in a headlock.

'Why couldn't you just be good?' I sob as I continue to squeeze my arm around her neck. 'Why couldn't you just sing...'

The Pica Explorer

Day six. Hour 08:15.

I sit with her, stroking her short hair and I notice how dirty it is. She hasn't had a wash for a few days. None of us have. We are both on the ground and her body is slumped onto my lap while I smooth her greasy fringe out of the way so that I can see her face properly. She looks like she is sleeping. Her body is cold and skinny. I can feel her shoulder blades digging into my thighs.

Looking around the empty room I am glad I am not by myself. It would be frightening being on the bottom of the ocean floor, trapped alone, but I am lucky – I have my Robin back.

It is clear I am going to die here but I have accepted it and am at peace. For the first time in my life I am where I belong and where I am meant to be. For all my life I've felt like a stranger walking the earth, like I don't belong. But here, with my little bird, I can at last be myself. My childhood was filled with sadness and fear but that has all melted away now.

I say a silent goodbye to Mummy and Olly. Olly was a mistake. It should never have happened. Who was I kidding? I was never going to escape my past and it was greedy to think I could go on and have a happy life. For so long I wanted to be like everyone else but now I know that was pointless and now I have accepted what I am. It doesn't matter that they are all dead. Perhaps I, too, am dead. Maybe I've never been alive. Maybe this is all just a dream and I am the figment of someone's twisted imagination. Perhaps this is just a story and I am a character playing a role. I don't know anymore.

Letting out a long sigh I slide Robin's head off my lap and get up to stretch. I am exhausted and thankful I don't have to fight anymore.

On a chair in the far corner I see a video camera and approach it. Picking it up I go and settle on another chair and set the camera up on the table, so that it is facing me.

It's unlikely we will ever be found but I now have an opportunity to set the record straight, so I look into the lens and begin to speak. The words pour out of me and I tell the camera everything. There should be a record of what happened here. It should not be lost.

Perhaps one day this vessel will be discovered, the bones of everyone on board lying scattered around. Maybe the sea will eventually eat through the walls and we will become one with the salt water. I don't know what will happen and there is painful bliss in the uncertainty, but what I do know is that I have a chance to set the record straight and I will tell my story and share the ugliness that I have suffered and been the cause of. Mummy set me on this course. There was never any way that I would escape my fate. She saw to that.

It occurs to me, for the very first time, that perhaps I am like her. She was cruel and sadistic and that is what I have become – but it is all her fault. If only she'd loved me. If only she hadn't brought Nick into our lives. If only she hadn't killed Robin. But there is little point crying over spilt milk. What's done is done and now I must accept what has happened.

Turning off the camera, I wrap it in a towel and put it in a cupboard, to keep it safe. At last there is a record and I feel better for expelling the truth. It came flooding out of me like a tidal wave and the fog from my mind has lifted for the first time since I can remember. No longer do I feel like a ghost watching the world turning around me. Now I am part of it and I can exist in the present.

Returning to Susie I bend down and squat on my heels. I no longer see a person. I see a bird. The feathers start to gently push their way through her skin, sprouting like flowers in spring. The place where her nose once was begins to transform into a perfect little beak. Rolling her onto her back I spread her arms out and watch the feathers grow out of her limbs. It is magical and I sit back, watching in awe as the transformation takes place in front of my eyes. Her wings are there now, returned to their rightful owner, and the memory of the broken little body I last saw on the kitchen floor, when I was a child, has faded into oblivion and been replaced by the marvel I see before me.

'You have your wings back, little bird.' Tears stream down my face. 'I fixed you.'

Just as I reach out to touch the miracle I hear a loud thud from somewhere in the distance and then the sound of heavy footsteps growing louder.

'No, no.' I cradle my head in my hands. 'Leave me alone.' The pain in my skull is instant and stabs like a knife. I begin to sweat and a violent wave of nausea hits me in the stomach.

Whimpering, I crawl towards my bird and rest my head on its chest. I can hear the heart beating and the life flowing through its veins.

'You are alive?' Lifting my head I look into its eyes, which have opened wide. The beak begins to move and as I watch I think my heart might explode in my chest. Its black eyes are staring. 'Come on, Robin, you can do it. Just sing. Sing one more time.' The giant sparrow tips its head back and opens its beak.

'*Hush, little baby, don't say a word.*' The tune carries around the room and the sound is the most beautiful thing I've ever heard. It is more than a song that I hear. It is a musical instrument playing. It speaks to my soul and cuts through the pain in my head. I am hypnotised by the beauty of the sound.

In the distance somewhere I hear banging on the door to the room I am in and a muffled voice calling out to me but I cannot make sense of the words.

'Keep singing, little bird.' I close my eyes and let the music travel through me. 'Keep singing.'

The Pica Explorer

Day six. Hour 08:30.

'Let me in.' I bang on the door with my fists. 'It's me, Luke! Come on. What's going on in there? I heard someone screaming.'

After trying for so long I managed to burst through the door that was keeping me trapped in the bunkroom. I can't believe they locked me in there.

I walked around looking for them but everywhere I went all I saw was death. Sam, Frank, Anya, they are all dead and I don't understand what has happened to these dudes.

It was when I heard someone call out that I knew I had to get out of there. I kicked and kicked until the door gave way. My foot really aches now but it hasn't stopped me looking for people. I know someone is alive. I heard them.

'Who's in there? Are you okay? What is going on?' Resting my tired head against the door, I struggle to hear. There is no sound coming from the room but I know there is someone in there. It has been locked from the inside.

'It's fine,' I tell them. 'I'm better now. I just freaked out a bit. You can trust me. Let me in, guys.' Still there is no response.

'You can't leave me out here.' The rage erupts from nowhere and I start slamming my hands against the door so hard that my palms begin to sting.

'Just fucking open the door!'

'Is that you, Luke?' A weak voice comes from inside the room.

'Yes, yes. Zara, is that you? Where's everyone else?'

'I'm scared, Luke. I don't understand what's going on.'

'It's okay. I'm here. Let me in.' I'm doing my best to sound calm even though that isn't how I feel.

'You'll hurt me.' Zara sounds childlike.

'No, no I won't. I promise. I just want to make sure you are all right. That's all.' Putting my ear against the cold door I try to listen better. 'Come on, Zara, it's okay. You can do it. Just open up. Please.'

'I can't.' I can hear that she has come closer to the door. 'Mummy won't let me.' There is something strange in her voice, something I don't recognise and it makes my blood run cold.

'Zara.' My voice remains calm but my body is shaking. 'If you don't open this fucking door I am going to smash it down. You have to the count of five before I start kicking.' Despite the throb in my foot I mean every word. 'Come on, Zara. I just want to talk to you.'

'You sound angry. I don't like it when people are angry.' Again, I can't help thinking she sounds like a kid and not the adult she is.

'I'm not angry.' I take a deep breath through my nose. 'But I need you to let me come in.'

On the other side of the door I hear movement. What is she up to in there? Then, to my amazement the door opens a crack. I have to control myself not to go bursting in but I remind myself I don't know what she's been through while I was shut in that room.

'There we go,' I encourage, 'not that difficult. Now, I'm going to come in, okay?'

I hear her scurry away and push on the door. Never could I have ever been prepared for the sight in the room.

On the floor, spread out, is Susie. She has been stripped naked and the skin from her body has been ripped away. The smell of the blood is all around. In a corner, Zara sits hugging her knees to her chest while she rocks on the spot humming a tune to herself.

'What the fuck happened?' I notice a splatter of blood across her cheek and all over her hands. She doesn't respond and keeps on humming.

I look around the room, still in shock. It is a bloodbath.

'Zara?' I choke, putting my hand over my mouth and falling to my knees with a thud.

Zara gets up and I see her clothes are soaked with blood. In her hand is a knife. She walks over to Susie as if she is strolling through a park and starts to hack away at her face.

Horrified, I can do nothing except watch while Zara sets to work butchering the body like it is a piece of meat. Still she is humming and I realise I know the song.

Unable to carry on sitting there, I manage to get up and stand. Taking clumsy steps towards Zara, I beg her to stop but it is like she can't hear me. She is in her own terrifying little world.

I try not to look at the mess that was once Susie, but I can't tear my eyes away. The closer I get I realise there is something odd about Susie's face. It looks strange and unlike her. Then I realise that it has pen marks all over it. Zara had been drawing on her. There are thick lines around her eyes and I can see that her hair has been hacked at. Clumps of hair have been cut away and her pale skull is showing through the bald patches.

'Why, Zara? Why did you do it? What is wrong with you?'

She turns to me and smiles and I see there is blood on her teeth.

'Have you been biting her?' The idea of it makes me feel sick.

'Do you like my picture?' She puts her head to one side and admires her work.

'You're mad. You're fucking sick!'

'Pretty bird.' Zara puts the knife down and picks up Susie's lifeless foot, which she holds against her bloody cheek while rubbing her face against it. Then the humming starts again.

I can't take this anymore. This nightmare has gone on long enough. Without thinking I slide the knife away from her. She doesn't seem to notice. She is too locked inside her own mad head.

Looking down at the horrific scene it dawns on me that Zara is the one who has killed them all. How she managed it I don't know, but I know for certain that it was her doing. Pity and disgust mingle and I don't know whether to laugh or to cry. This sad, mental woman has been the cause of all these deaths. Her madness has killed innocent people and now only she and I remain.

My eyes wander around the room and I remember we aren't getting off this thing. I'm trapped with a deranged killer and I remember how it all began, how we all came together to create something that was meant to be good. How did it all go so wrong? But then I realise that the moment the sub sunk we were all doomed. None of us were ever going to escape with our lives intact, which makes what she has done even more pointless.

I look at the corpse lying spread out on the floor. Poor Susie.

I can't stay in this room anymore. I need to get out. I can't breathe and I stumble away from the scene of the massacre.

Zara turns her head slowly, like a doll, and watches as I back away.

'Where are you going?' Her voice is higher than normal and she sounds so innocent.

'I erm, have to go for a piss.' I have to get away from this woman. 'I need the bog.' I will say anything to get away.

'You should stay with us, Luke.' She gets up, still covered in Susie's blood, and begins walking towards me. There is a vacant look in her eyes that scares me to my core.

'Stay there, Zara. Don't come any closer.'

She's not listening and continues to take slow steps. I have two choices. I either try and run or deal with this face on. But there is nowhere to run. There is no exit.

Lying on a table is a large metal torch. Without thinking I pick it up.

'I'm warning you, Zara. Stay back.' But like a zombie she floats closer and closer.

Closing my eyes I hold the torch up and swing it against her head, which makes a cracking sound before popping like a watermelon. I can't look at her twitching body on the floor. I leave the room, pulling the door closed behind me.

There is nowhere for me to go so I walk aimlessly through the sub towards the control room. It is one of the few places left that isn't stained with blood. Stepping over Sam and Frank's bodies I try to ignore the rank smell that hangs in the air.

Once in the control room I close the door and sit in the gloom, staring out into the black water knowing that I am going to die a killer and no one will ever know what took place down here.

Leaning back in the chair I look around at the dials and control panel and wish there were a magic button that could take me to the surface and away from this place of horrors.

As I flop back into my chair something catches my eye. In a small box up high I see the word SOS written in white on the glass front of a box.

Standing up, I make a fist and break the glass to remove the box. Inside I find three flares and a flare gun. It makes me laugh. Breaking into hysterical laughter I double over, still holding the rescue equipment. The irony isn't lost on me.

I don't cry often but I can't stop myself and after letting it all out I feel tired and close my eyes. I'm going to rest now. There isn't anything else left to do and as I close my eyes I quickly start to slip into a sleep. Somewhere in the background I hear a faint crackle. It sounds like a radio and I welcome the dream that promises to drag me under. I hear it again, the crackling sound, and open one eye.

Crrrkkk, crrrrrkkkkk.

I am sitting bolt upright and my eyes are open wide now.

Crrrrrkkkkk. Crrrkk. Crrrrkkk.

The noise is coming from the radio.

'Hello, hello?' I yell into the microphone. 'Is anyone there?' It falls silent again. I hit the microphone with the palm of my hand. 'Hello?'

Crrrrkkkk. Crrrrrkkkkk.

'This is The Pica Explorer. Can you hear me?' I choke on my hope. The quiet is unbearable.

'This... crrrrrkkkk... I crrkkkkk... SAS crrrkkkkk.' I've never been so happy to hear something so unintelligible.

'Yes! Yes. I'm down here!' My voice cracks just like the radio.

Crrrrkkkk. Then there is a long squeal from the radio before I am plunged back into silence again.

'Hello?' Talking into the microphone, I long to hear another voice again but there is no response. 'Hello!' I scream. 'Hello, hello, hello! Is there anyone there?'

After a few moments of total quiet I get up and I start to punch the buttons on the panel in front of me repeatedly until my knuckles split. I hate this submarine.

Crrrkkkk. I freeze, wanting to hear the sound again.

Crrrrrkkkkkkk.

'Come in, crrrkkkkk,'

'Yes, yes, hello.' I hold the microphone as close to my mouth as I can.

'What is your position? Repeat, what is your position? Crrrkkkk.' The sound of the man's voice is like music to my ears.

'Repeat, crrrrrkkkkkkkk, what, ccrrrrrk, is your position?'

Hanging my head, I allow myself a smile.

Crrrrrkkkkk.

'Pica Explorer, come in crrkkk, this is crrkkkk… what is your position?'

Leaning over the mic I look out into the black water.

'I don't know.'

THE END

Acknowledgements

I'd like to take a moment to acknowledge that this is a strange book. It asks that you stretch your imagination and remove yourself from reality and I accept that this may not please some of you for that reason, but I wanted to delve into fiction in its purest form. This is the result.

Having said that, every novel I've written has always been inspired, one way or another, by real-life events, often reported in the news and this story was inspired by the tragic real-life events that saw an Argentinian submarine disappear with forty-four people on board. The thought of being trapped on board a vessel at the bottom of the ocean filled me with fear. That was the birth of this book.

I would like to take this opportunity to thank people who have helped make this book possible.

Firstly, thanks to Emma Pullar for her insight on a difficult subject. Les Morris for his unending knowledge about submarines. Andrew Barrett for his advice on decomposition. To my wonderful BETA readers – Anita Waller, Emma Pullar, Mark Tilbury and my mother. You all helped to tighten this novel and I am forever grateful.

A special mention for Alexina Golding who BETA read the book and used her eagle eye to help improve the narrative.

To Clare Law who always manages to polish my work so that it is readable.

For my children who put up with me and my husband who encourages and forces himself to read my books, even when he is up to his eyeballs with work. To Sarah Hardy who does a wonderful job arranging the publicity and Sumaira Wilson who, with her magic hands, has the ability to turn a Word document into a real-life book.

For all the bloggers who take time out of their busy lives to help promote the writers they love, I take my hat off to you.

To Susan Hunter who is a wonderful woman and I would like to mention her just because I can!

To the amazing people who run book clubs, libraries and online groups, and who have a passion for reading, you make it all worthwhile.

Finally, I'd like to thank Amazon and all the Kindle readers out there for giving me the career of my dreams.

Anything is possible. Dedicated to the families and the forty-four crew members of The ARA San Juan, which disappeared without a trace on November 15th 2017.

9 781912 604258